HOPED REALITY

Hoped Reality-What if it exists?
Edited & Compiled by Bhavya Rao
Print Edition

First Published in India in 2021
Inkfeathers Publishing
New Delhi 110095

Copyright © Inkfeathers Publishing, 2021
Cover Design © 2021 Inkfeathers Publishing
Cover Image © laskoart from Freepik.com

www.inkfeathers.com

HOPED REALITY

WHAT IF IT EXISTS?

Edited & Compiled by

Bhavya Rao

Inkfeathers Publishing

DISCLAIMER

The anthology "Hoped Reality–What If It Exists?" is a collection of 19 stories by 19 authors who belong to different parts of the globe. The anthology editor and the publisher have edited the content provided by the co-authors to enhance the experience for readers and make it free of plagiarism as much as possible. Unless otherwise indicated, all the names, characters, objects, businesses, places, events, incidents- whether physical/non-physical, real/unreal, tangible/ intangible in whatsoever description used in this book are either the product of the author's imagination or used in a fictitious manner. Any resemblance to actual persons, objects, entities, living or dead, or actual events is purely coincidental. The stories published in this book are solely owned by their respective authors and are no way intended to hurt anyone's religious, political, spiritual, brand, personal or fanatic beliefs and/or faith, whatsoever.

In case, any sort of plagiarism is detected in the stories within this anthology or in case of any complaints or grievances or objections, neither the anthology editor, nor the publisher are to be held responsible for any such claims. The author(s) who holds the rights to the story, shall be held responsible, whatsoever.

CO-AUTHORED BY

Celestina Copil ~ Urvi Dhruva ~ Isheta Boruah ~ Prathibha Srinivasan ~ Shubha Pai ~ Adithya AJ ~ Shivangi Gupta ~ Akshitha Gajanand ~ Siddhanth Raju ~ Amy Grace ~ C.L. Williams ~ Harsha Shinde ~ Raga Lahari ~ Bibin K Babu ~ Nikita K ~ Pravallika Kadiri ~ Rasagya Gade ~ Tushar Dudhade ~ Aryaman Kumar

CONTENTS

ABOUT THE EDITOR

Bhavya Rao

Bhavya is that one dreamer who'd procrastinate even while dreaming. She suffers from a syndrome of crying the whole night after finishing each book she picks once in 3 days. She knows just the drop in the ocean where she deep dives into that drop for ages. She has a special eye for unnoticed things and hence the theme of the book. To conclude you'd like to hate and love her equally because she's just the right amount of mess and art in this racing world.

EDITOR'S NOTE

Do we realise that we often create opposite scenarios of the reality we face? As a kid, I always wished for things to happen in a certain way which was quite opposite from reality. This made me wonder if there was any possibility that there existed some other place where things were different and satisfying my curiosity, unlike reality. With time, grew my imagination and so did my curiosity for this thought.

And that's where it all started. I wondered if there existed any more peculiar curiosities just like mine. And there grew my curiosity to know them all. I knew there were many out there struggling with their unrealistic imagination to be poured out but couldn't find the way to let it out.

This book is a compilation of all the imaginations sprung from those silent curious minds hidden under our cover of reality. Each story in the book has no real connectivity with the other and that's the whole purpose of it. But in the end, you just know you were connected to all, not just one. While I read each story, it reflected that a part of me has also wondered the same at a certain point of time. The toughest job was selecting the order of stories because each one felt interesting enough to go first but then to my confused mind, this order seemed the best. But honestly, it's totally up to you which story you want to dive in first.

To my readers, while you read this, you're going to travel to places, and you'll know it. So go ahead grab a snack and travel to different dimensions.

1

TO KNOW WHAT A BENCH IS

BY CELESTINA COPIL

We are all sitting on, next to and in front of a bench. Each one of the five of us is very proud of his conquered spot. Mine is on a stump, where I was seated only by the grace of the tenants, some kind ants, which swiftly departed at my imminent approach.

'Look at this bench, broken and scribbled and disheveled and—' 'Yes, those vandals!'

My friends are now arguing over which direction benches should face, the alley or the trees; and I must confess that this topic is not of any particular interest for me. I notice a ladybug on my shirt, a little one, with only two dots on its back. I put it on my finger and start watching it traversing my palm from one end to the other.

Up until now, we had been chatting about nothing and everything, cutting each other short to make jokes, fighting to tell a better story than the previous speaker. Words had been flowing back and forth like an angry swarm of bees and sounds of laughter had been swinging the flowery branches of chestnut above us. But now, I observe that, for no apparent reason, the otherwise loud conversation has stopped for a moment. I begin pondering how there is nothing more beautiful than just standing next to your darlings. Quiet. Being aware of their presence. Rejoicing at the thought of their existence, which so, fortunately, happens to be intertwined with yours. In moments like this, I feel that a glance would be enough to tell the whole heart, words only serving as a disruption of the moment.

As I am taking my eyes off the ladybug, I can see the others looking away, pretending to be absorbed by the sight of the other people passing by, desperately trying to think of something to talk about. Situations like this never fail to amuse me. 'What is this need for a constant exchange of words?' I think to myself. We always say that we can't wait to see each other, and yet, when we meet, we open our mouths way before our eyes.

I am enjoying the silence, as it has brought with itself the occasion to experience the cozy feeling of just not being alone. For once, the others also seem to accept the situation, succeeding to make it less awkward by doing so. I am dwelling in the silent wish that moments like this would happen more often.

I remember how, on my way to meet them, I spent precious minutes thinking about how to respond to the inevitable, ever present questions such as "How are you?" and "What have you been doing lately?" Now with the questions in front of me, I find myself presented with a cruel choice. The first option would be to tell a plain boring or even—why not say it—unpleasant to hear the truth. The second would be to deflect the questions with humour. I don't even know why I bother to consider the former, as it has been clear for me for a long time that a joke is always a better-received answer. And the pathetic thing would be that despite valuing silence so much, I had an unnecessarily long list of emergency questions in the back of my head in case the silence ever became unbearable. This would have been a good time to put them to use, but still, remaining true to my values—and this somehow made me feel better—I don't step in to revive the conversation.

Slowly and somewhat imperceptibly, the silence departs along with the discomfort it had brought to the others. We resume our talking. Thinking of the last few hours which we have spent together, I am amazed at the realization that I can't—and couldn't, not even with a gun to my head—remember what we could have possibly talked about. There are one or two things that are still lingering in my mind, which I presume to be the most important things discussed today. But could it be that we met and spent an entire evening together and there were only two things worth talking about? What about the other thirty thousand words we've spoken? Were they voiced in vain? Wasted away? If only we'd stop talking unnecessarily! Is it such a daring wish to have?

Perhaps, in a parallel universe, there are no words.

Perhaps, in that parallel universe, when people meet, they look in each other's eyes without feeling the burden to make conversation.

Perhaps, in that parallel universe, people admire paintings and don't have to write entire essays to understand art and feel moved by it. They face the sun and let the rays softly caress their skin without having to comment on the fineness of the day.

Perhaps, in that parallel universe, people do not have to endure all the tedious exchanges of words on frivolous topics. They do not have to wait until reaching a certain level of friendship, when it is finally appropriate to address one's fears, impossible desires and hidden feelings, as it is the case now.

Without the anxious "What should I say next?" thought, a true connection is attained, in which there is no need to express feelings verbally, for the others can read them in the eye. And when those eyes cry, they are met not with generic comforting words, but with patient silence and an understanding embrace.

Perhaps, in that parallel world, silence is always both the question and the answer.

I am finally home, in my little bedroom, feeling a little tired of it all—stories, laughs, sounds, people. I am quite glad that the day is over and that I am alone again.

The moon rays coming through the window are competing with the lamp on the bureau. I turn it off and let the room bask in the moonlight. I am glad to observe that—finally—our hard of hearing neighbours are not watching television late at night, as they usually do. The street is still, no arguing drunkards, no loud teenagers. I feel the corners of the room are coming closer to the center and now the ceiling is almost touching the crown of my head… The scene becomes surreal, and I find myself having a sudden urge to go outside.

The loud squeaking of the wooden door as I open it is the only thing I can hear. I take a final look over my shoulder at the room I am leaving behind and I see the long curtains gently sweeping the floor. 'The wind is blowing in the room,' is all I can think of. The image persists in my mind as I am taking the first step on the wet pavement. Has it been raining? 'It's possible,' I think to myself and continue watching downward at my feet.

I observe that I am shivering, skin full of tiny bumps. Surely that must have happened before. I take my eyes off the ground and I see someone walking toward me. I am wondering if the passerby had ever experienced this awful sensation—what is it called, again? I'd like to ask what his thoughts on it are, other than having the natural need to put something on.

Now, looking at this stranger, I realize that all human beings must be having lives as complex as my own —which is a mesmerizing thing to think about. Peeking into someone else's mind must be an awesome experience. My insistent look goes unnoticed, so I stop and grab the person by the arm. Eyebrows go into a furious frown, the muscles around a roman nose contract in a terrible grimace, as if the person is one second away from biting me. I retract my arm, profoundly shaken by this. Before I can join my palms into an apology, the person is already lost into the night.

I continue my aimless strolling through the dark alleys. Above me, the faint flickers we call stars are winking at me. Are they trying to tell me something? I take immense pleasure in admitting I won't ever know. But I wish I could speak their language.

Not long afterwards, I see two people sitting on a bench, holding hands. The night is uncomfortably quiet as I am approaching the two. 'A lovely couple', I think to myself, 'so quiet.' She is fidgeting in her seat, looking as if she wants something, why isn't she voicing it over? He looks at her, he is curious, he doesn't understand. He gets up and gestures towards his left, in a questioning manner. 'Do you want us to go?' he seems to be asking. They start walking, she smiles and closes her eyes for a moment—a sign of gratitude, as I understood it.

They must have been an odd mute couple. If she desired to leave, why didn't she signal it? With her hands, if in no other way...

I start remembering a cold day in January, thirty frozen

breaths barely warming the classroom. The voice of our teacher reverberated in the room despite our constant rustling whispers. The back of the chamber, where I sat, was a truly strategic point in that, from there, I could see everything except the writing on the blackboard. My interest in the lesson was almost non-existent and my attention completely elsewhere. After finding some pencil shavings that I suppose were left there by accident, I started running them one by one on my notebook with my finger, drawing curved lines and circles and shapes. I would have done anything to escape the boredom.

'The definition of the term is, and you shall remember this...' the teacher started.

Suddenly, the subject became interesting. Words have always been a fascinating topic for me, in whichever form they appeared: spoken or implied, written or in the form of thoughts, in books and conversations...

'A term consists of three parts: the linguistic—that is, the word or the expression; the ontological—referring to the object itself; and the cognitive—the notion it conveys.'

It was simple—and obvious once it was explained to me in this manner. I started thinking of how we use words to assign objects a name, a meaning. We, as humans, looked at a tree, named it 'tree' and from there on, regardless of formal differences, we knew what a tree was, and we could recognize one when we saw it. And we could go to a person and pronounce the word 'tree' and that person would know exactly what we are trying to say.

'Language!' I thought. 'What a marvelous invention, that is!'

After walking mindlessly for who knows how long, I find myself in a place I cannot name. The sight makes me feel good, although I cannot understand why. I cannot name the feeling, either. I continue looking, but things make less and less sense. I stop. Finally, I find myself not knowing what I am looking at.

The place seems familiar, not because I have been here before, but because it resembles other places. Is this place... somehow related to the others I am picturing in my head right now? Are all of those places the same thing...manifested differently?

What a strange thought! Each place must be distinct.

I sit down and concentrate on the view again. The same feeling of unexplained pleasure, a certain warmth, is filling my chest. I began thinking of a way to share this experience with someone else later. But that someone would want to know where I was, how did it look like, what did I feel...What could I do to convey this image? I could point out to my heart and smile and the others would know I was feeling good. But how to make him understand where I was and what I was seeing? How can I make him think about the same thing as I am thinking?

I see movement. I am watching cautiously, trying to assess if the motion could mean that there is danger nearby. Now, my mind is blank except for an instinctual desire to survive.

A form distinguishes itself from the dark. Its dimensions are approximately equal to my body. I exhale relieved at the thought that I could, at least, survive an eventual fight.

Still, what is this form? I look down to my body, I compare it to that of the forms... The similarities are striking. Could it be... me? Or perhaps, my reflection? But no, it is moving independently. And there are a few differences; longer hair, different skin color... Could we still be the same thing, in a way? Similarly, to the place that seemed to resemble others I've seen before, this form could also be, in essence, the same thing with ...me. And I am...

What am I? I forgot. There was a name for a thing like me, wasn't it? Where is that name gone? How can I exist when I don't know what I am?

I look around. There are things around me, but it seems I forgot their names too.

A sudden memory resurfaces, and I find myself re-experiencing a scene that happened earlier.

My insistent look goes unnoticed. I stop and grab the person by the arm.

That is it! The person. A human, I now remember. I am a human, and this form in front of me is one, too. That is it! We are the ontological part of the word, isn't it? Now I remember; behind all people, there is an essence which makes us call them 'human', even if they are distinct objects...

I feel something pulling me out of my memory and out of my mind. I try to resist, but finally, I abandon the thought about the word 'human' and I am sitting down again.

I look around. What are all these in front of me? I don't know. I only know that I need to survive.

At the moment I am safe, but something is unsettling about not understanding one's surroundings. There must be something wrong. I can feel it. Things have not always been this way, isn't it?

I visualize myself sitting here forever not knowing what is wrong with me, and the thought—even if it is kind of undefined and formless—of an eternal state of not understanding is paralyzing. I am aware of growing fear in my chest.

Why is this happening? I don't know.

What am I missing? I forgot.

What did I lose? I will, perhaps, never find out.

I gradually become aware of my surroundings; the reverie is over, time starts flowing again, I am back on my stump, the stump from where the ants left.

'Words!' I find myself saying, to the other's surprise. They do not understand what I am trying to say. And I don't, either. It was only the first thought that came to mind.

I look at them. They are in front of me, they are sitting on and around the bench. I am looking at it and it takes me a moment to become aware that, well, I know what a bench is.

'I know what a bench is, isn't it amazing?', I voiced the thought without hesitation, again.

I get a few laughs from my friends who are now teasing me about taking so long to discover such a mundane thing.

How easy it is for them to laugh! They have no idea what it means not to know what a bench is.

2

RATHER HEAR THAN THERE

BY URVI DHRUVA

Maybelle took a deep breath and muttered to herself, "I can do this." She wondered for the billionth time how she got roped into this instead of spending a lazy evening in PJs, lying on the couch doing nothing till the point she could count herself as a part of the furniture. But she knew that the 'being furniture' practice session could happen another time. After another 2 minutes of a self-pep talk and fixing her brown hair in her 'work mode on' bun, she walked into the room. In the room, everyone was waiting rather impatiently for her. She smiled sheepishly, realizing that the pep-talk made her late, and took one of the last two chairs placed in a circle.

There were 5 other people apart from her and she decided to study them, trying to get an idea of what she would be dealing with today. A woman was wearing enough clothes to be toasty in Antarctica. While Maybelle was not exactly a fashionista and preferred a white t-shirt and jeans, even she cringed at the outfit that the lady had decided to wear. This lady wore a polka dot yellow tank top, the kind of yellow that hurt your eyes, with a tiger stripes cardigan with pink hot shorts and neon leg warmers which had pom-poms on them. Maybelle closed her eyes for a second, giving them momentary relief from the burst of colors, and decided to look at someone else.

To the left of 'layer lady', there was a young boy who seemed to be the age of 10-11 years. Was he lost or someone's kid? He looked bored and was playing with the oversized sleeve of his shirt. It looked like he was trying to fit in but was failing miserably, both in his clothes and the room. Next to him was a girl in her late teens, going through what seemed like a goth phase. She was dressed in black from head to toe. She was busy texting someone on her phone, unaware of the people in the room with her. She had a tattoo on her forearm, a drawing of Morticia Addams with a red rose. The rose was the only color present on her. The guy next to Maybelle seemed to be from a wealthy background. He wore a grey suit which looked tailor-made. He kept fixing his already perfect hair staring blatantly at the goth girl. Maybelle prayed he was not a creep and if he were, that he wouldn't notice her. Was it too late to shift to the empty seat away from the creep?

The goth girl looked like she kept a knife in her shoe so she should be alright. The lady on the right of Mr. Creepy kept pulling down her dress and fixing her hair. She was trying to start a conversation with Mr. Creepy who was completely ignoring her. The lady finally seemed to give up, looking at her hands in her lap, fidgeting with her bracelet. Maybelle decided that none of these people were going to take an initiative so she decided she would.

She got up clearing her throat and said, "Hi guys!" I think we should begin this meeting and not wait any longer." Mr. Creepy laughed and quipped, "Yes, finally! Who wants to take off their clothes first?" Maybelle rolled her eyes, already wanting this nightmare to end. "Let's introduce ourselves and go round the circle." The layer lady suggested. "I will start – My name is Sarah." Sarah nudged the goth girl who glared but reluctantly kept her phone on her lap. "Beth." That was all she said. The kid politely asked if he could go next. Maybelle nodded and he beamed "Hi everyone, my name is Derek, and I am 10 years old." Maybelle smiled at him, silently appreciating his good manners.

Mr. Creep decided it was his turn to shine "Hey my name is Aaron, but you can call me tonight." And winked. Maybelle wondered if that line had worked on anyone since, let's see, never. Sarah the 'layer lady' looked equally disgusted. Ms. Desperate, however, blushed furiously and mumbled, "Hello, I am...uh...Evianna...but I go by Eve." "Can I be the Adam to your Eve?" Mr. Creepy joked. This led to Derek questioning him "But I thought your name was Mr. Aaron, that's what you said, right?" Maybelle suppressed her smile while Mr. Creep groaned and decided wisely, for once to not comment. Maybe Mr. Cringey is a more appropriate nickname, Maybelle thought. Maybelle looked over to the empty chair beside her and wondered if the person was coming or not.

Maybelle looked away and said, "Hi, I am Maybelle." Goth girl hesitated but then spoke up "So Maybelle, why don't you tell us your story?" Maybelle squeaked "um me? I don't know if I am ready to speak yet..." Eve smiled sympathetically at her and volunteered to speak instead. Maybelle shot her a look of gratitude, feeling relieved. Now in the spotlight suddenly, Eve took a deep breath and started, "I don't think I am good enough sometimes. I try hard and it feels like people with no efforts seem to fare better than me. It's like I am stuck in the loop of impressing people, trying to win them and fulfill their expectations of me, of who I should be. I am so tired of proving that I am good enough all the damn time!" There was silence but you could sense the surprise everyone felt for the woman who looked so put together but was falling apart inside. But then again, do we care to know about people? "I read that you should believe in yourself, even if no one else does because, in the end, you are all that material" the kid blurted. "Kid, I think you mean you are all that matters" chuckled Sarah "and you are very bright."

The awkwardness dissipated from the room and everyone relaxed a little. Sarah considered something for a moment and then shook her head "I will go next. I am very passionate, but I never get the attention I want. I get all these ideas and I am never considered, and I agree that my ideas are a bit "out of the norm" but aren't these ideas the ones that help you step out of this format box people keep living in? I am just pushed to a corner and it makes me so frustrated that I am not even valued…" Beth snickered "Oh, are your feelings hurt by a bunch of other people who don't care about you? How sad." And eye-rolled when Maybelle sent her a pointed look. "Sorry, I didn't mean to hurt you… I am not good with emotions; I am very uncomfortable. It's not who I am, I just think through stuff logically so…" "If you think logically and have no problems, why are you here then?" questioned Eve. "Because logic isn't always the answer. Humans aren't machines and everyone isn't like me, so I end up hurting them rather than helping them" shrugged Beth. Goth girl is more mature than most adults, Maybelle mentally noted.

"So, Maybelle, do you have a solution for hottie over there?" asked Mr. Rich Creep. Maybelle stared at him as if he was an alien. Did he think she was secretly God and possessed powers to create world peace?! Beth sent a death glare to Mr. Cringey. "Am I supposed to have solutions to all your problems?" questioned Maybelle. Now Mr. Cringey looked at her like she was a talking rabbit. "Well, we are here because of you." What did that mean? The last time she checked, she didn't open Pandora's box and curse all of humanity to have problems in life. "I am confused... I thought you were here for your problems." "Our problems are more intertwined than you can think." Sarah explained. Maybelle was flabbergasted "I have never met or seen any of you people ever before, I don't know you!" Sarah smiled ominously, "Oh but sweetie we know you..." Maybelle wondered if this was a stalker's meet and she was their unfortunate victim. Were they going to kill her and she is going to end up on news as the unfortunate (read dumb) woman who walked right into the room filled with her murderers? Maybelle sent a silent prayer to God and promised she would never do anything bad ever if she was saved this one time.

Eve raised her voice, "Enough, don't freak her out! We all know how good she gets at shutting herself out."

"What? I don't... How would you know anything about me!?" stammered Maybelle. Aaron (aka Mr. Cringey) put his hand on his forehead, pretending to think, and said, "Yeah you are right, we don't know anything about you just like we don't know anything about that cute neighbour incident or how you trip every time you walk, like seriously do you not know how to walk?!" "Or how you felt on Wednesday or how you think about "You know who" any chance you get but you push away those wistful thoughts." Beth added. "Are you guys mind readers or something?! Whatever it is, stop because it's creepy." "We aren't but you know who we are, stop denying it "Sarah spoke up. "What, are you people in my head?" Maybelle laughed. "Technically we are you, just different parts of you" Sarah said seriously.

Maybelle waited for a long minute, expecting to be told she was part of a prank show or she would wake up to her alarm and this was just a bizarre dream she would forget in 10 minutes. When nothing of that sort happened, she swallowed and said "I am a normal person who doesn't have any major problems. This is technically not possible." "We agree, but it's true that you have normal problems, things everybody goes through. You seem to be unable to deal with them and just choose to shut yourself off pretending to be blind to them as if they are people who will get offended and go away because you are ignoring them. "Beth explained. "If I ignore you guys, will you people go away?" Maybelle muttered to herself. Beth smiled and added," What you don't understand is that these little things build-up, so we collectively decided to hold a meeting before you explode or worse, Sarah takes over all of your personality. In Sarah's words, this is an extraordinary solution to your ordinary problem." Maybelle goes to protest that she isn't someone who loses control but remembers the incident where she screamed at a barista for messing up her coffee order one day. In her defense, it was a particularly stressful week.

Maybelle sighed "No offense to Sarah but I don't want that to happen, so what should we do?" "Great, accepting that you have a problem is the first step towards problem-solving. Now can you identify what personality we each are and understand how you deal with stuff?" Aaron suggested. "Um okay, Aaron is sadly my awkward version, trying to change the topic of a conversation sometimes. I am so awkward that making situations awkward makes me feel better, I think. Is there a separate meaning to your age and gender or is my mind all age-inclusive like a family restaurant?" Maybelle asked dryly. "See you are doing it again. Why do you want to change the topic sometimes?" pushed Aaron.

"Because it's easier than dealing with the problem causing me pain. And it's great because the bad attempt of humour is ironically a great distraction and people jump on judging that, forgetting what they wanted to talk about." Maybelle admitted. "You are doing great; I am proud of you. As for your question, everything has a meaning, it just depends which way you can interpret it." Informed Derek. Maybelle wondered how this kid was a part of her because he seemed so enlightened and she was clueless about so many things." Derek laughed while Eve said "The thing is most of the time the solutions are simple. People always know what the right thing is. It's only the problems which are complicated." Of course, they can read her thoughts, they were literally in her head. "Maybe in an alternate universe, we might just be voices in people's heads and they might need to go to someone to help deal with it." Sarah pondered out loud. Everyone looked at her but wisely chose not to question further.

"So, is this an intervention or therapy or am I so hungry that I am hallucinating? I knew switching to the salad for lunch was a terrible idea," Maybelle spoke in a serious tone, more to herself than the others in the room. "All we want is for you to acknowledge what you go through. Don't, what is it that those kids say, boo us?" Eve looked at Beth for help. "Ghost, not boo." Beth deadpanned. "Yes, as long as you can acknowledge your feelings, we won't have to hold this intervention for you." Eve promised. "Honestly, I would choose voices over you people ganging up on me here." Maybelle commented. "Oh honey, it's not a great idea because you can escape from us in the room but how do you escape from the people literally in your head? So be nice to us or we might start popping up at places to make sure you don't ghost us."

Sarah replied. "I could escape?! Why didn't you tell me this beforehand?" Maybelle screamed. "You already knew you could leave anytime none of us tied you or something, drama queen. You chose to sit here because it is the right thing to do." Beth commented, picking up her phone. "She gets the drama from me. Mommy is so proud, sweetie." Sarah sniffed. "Oh, who is this last chair for?" Maybelle questioned. "That's for old Crispy." Eve replied. Before Maybelle could say anything an elderly guy, easily in his 50s barged into the room panting "Sorry guys, I am late, I kind of got... "LOST!" all the personalities replied while Mr. Crispy smiled sheepishly. "I am the side of your personality who-" "Zones out, got it" Maybelle acknowledged.

Maybelle smiled at everyone, who were all sides of herself. Was saying bye even appropriate considering the fact they were a part of her, she considered internally. Maybelle woke up the next morning, wondering if what happened last night happened or not. She opened her door to get the newspaper. She remembered what had happened last week and walked up to her neighbour's door and rang the bell. A cute guy opened the door, and when he saw Maybelle surprise was evident in his eyes. "Um hi, I am sorry to disturb you. I wanted to apologize for wow, this is tough, running away from you last week, I uh accept your offer for the date if it still stands. I am just awkward when it comes to people and expressing stuff, you know." Maybelle swore she heard a chuckle and a bunch of "Atta girl, get that cutie." Hm, must be a figment of her imagination. The guy just grinned at her, "Sure, I thought you weren't interested. Do you have any suggestions where we could go for dinner?" Maybelle looked at the newspaper and saw attached to it a pamphlet for a waterpark at her doorstep with the tagline- "Fun for all ages" and smiled to herself and said, "It would be better if we go to a casual place. I am very clumsy."

3

WHERE ALL THE MINDS GO?

BY ISHETA BORUAH

Prologue

It is an estimation that space stretches about 93 billion light-years, which is again an estimation, as a human being we can envisage how vast the chances of the existence of extraterrestrial beings can be on the other side of the universe.

23,000 light-years away from the Milky Way Galaxy, exists a huge black hole, which succumbs almost all the particles of luminescence and if anyone can escape through the magnetic force and travels to the other side of the black hole by bending space and time, the person can directly be linked to the disparate point in space-time and pushing them to the alternate parallel terrestrial or alternate universe and from the exact point just 23,000 light-years away exist 'Xeone' one of the planets amidst billion unexplored Multiverses. Xeone covers 24,230,000 sq km approximately to the size of present-day North America of Earth. The habitats of Xeone are called Xeonites.

UNO

The fascinating exponent of Xeonites is that they have a

sectional division amongst them, and these sectional divisions are known as 'Partitio'. Each Partitio are divided into three sects Core,

Infirmi and Externus. The three sectional divisions – Partitio, vary distinctively from each other, having their jurisdictional limitation over Xeone. Each of the Partitio is confined to their own ruled out areas where the residents belonging to each sectional division reside. The sects where the residents of Core reside are the ones who have the undertaking to provide revenues to all the habitats of Xeonites. Since the residents of Core are relatively wealthy and provide, they control over the working of the other two sects i.e. Infirmi and Externus.

What makes these individuals the resident of Core is that each resident has inheritance and ability to harness, the Psychic Powers. The three most important Core Residents are:

Clairvoyants – they are the people who have the inherited ability to gain information about the physical event, object or person through extrasensory perception, they work in the department of forecasting disasters. The following residents are the Teleports – they are the ones who can bend space-time and light to travel from one distance to another, Telepaths - are other sects who work along with Teleports who can harness the energy from the black hole which is harnessed into full potential when passed through the 'Teleknosis' a power harnessing machinery which can only be generated by the Telepaths' 'high vibration-al mutts' which are infused into their heart, and when the low vibration-al and un-reactive 'Neutrinos' from black holes are harnessed by the Teleports and passed through 'Teleknosis' they become highly reactive with the Xeone's atoms causing them to split open a space-time and light bending portal which enables teleportation to the rich commoners.

Teleportation is usually used for:

a) Corporal Punishment to offenders or the incapable residents of Xeone.

b) Business deals in outer space.

c) Luxury holiday travels by the rich.

d) Emergency evacuation which has happened once in the billionth Xeonite years.

The presiding next most important resident of Core is the Mediumship or the Channelers – they provide justice to the residents of all the three Partitio through their means of communicating to the spirits in courts where the victim spirit (if dead) and the accused is called upon to solve the matter through Sub - Channelers to mediate the case in the Evelance Court of Justice and the judgement of the Mediumship is written by the Remote – Writers who through them

Psychokinetic - sensing abilities can manipulate the matter of Xeone and can move objects like pens or inks without touching them and the pen draws its course on its own when ordered by the Remote – Writers.

Infirmi

You know, in the course of existence some things are inevitable, for example falling on the ground or spiralling towards unexpected events in your life that you could never predict?

The residents of Xeonites saw an unbecoming event taking place approximately 100 Xeonite years ago, you might call it an inexplicable disease or a call from someone from the other side of the unknown. The people of Xeonite began to experience, might be called it as Psychogenic Mutation. There was havoc everywhere as some residents were not being able to control their psychic energy, the Psychokinetics were not able to contain themselves, due to the error in their Psychogenic matter they were creating massive kinetic energy balls without their control over it.

The ones who were Intuitive their brain wires were fired - up at spot due to over precognitive thoughts which they had no control. The Teleports without their will of force were teleporting themselves to unknown eras and events and returning to the point of the destination where they left, half of the population were as if going through a plaque in their genes which were controlling them. At that moment, an Institution called by the Core (which later became the part of Partitio) set up Infirmi Facility House, where the residents who are going through Psychogenic Mutation will be tested and cured in the Infirmi Facility House and as it contained one-fourth of the area of Xeonite, Infirmi became the second Partition.

A Beginning or an End?

The solution to new problems is also the creation of new problems.

Externus

What happens to the ones who are unable to cope up with the tides of forces of the Psychogenic Mutation? That is what the member of the Core tried to uncover. Containing a population which is going haywire due to the mutation cannot be conserved. Around 20,000 residents form the habitats of

Partitio. They are the ones who meet the fate of never finding the cure. It was set up when a total of 2,400 psychogenic mutation attacks were reported, and 500 residents each in a batch-wise were treated. The ones who got cured and retained their psychic stability were sent back to Core.

When the Mutation feeds into half of the DNA there is no retention of the psychic ability they ever possessed, they assert back to being a mundane being, unable to cope with the residents of Core. These residents are forced to do menial work which would give off a lot of labour if a resident of Core engages them with.

The people from Externus are sold to one another as slaves, are used as a medium of entertainment, sex slaves or for cleaning the parameters of living spaces of the residents of

Exinite. They are meant to stay in compact and unhealthy living spaces, throwing them away from the main bustling area of Xeone.

The ones who deny obeying the rules from the authorities from the Core are slewed from their living spaces, taken to the Infirmi Facility House, they are showered by psycho - powered android to avoid physical contact by the facilitators, clothed in new attires and are taken to the Teleportation Room. The Teleportation room contains one of the perplexing inventions of the Xeonite, the 'Teleknosis' powered and harnessed by the teleports and the telepaths.

The sufferers of the Psychogenic Mutation are then scathed away from near Telekinesis where Teleports can harness the energy from the dark matter of black hole which is harnessed into full potential when passed through 'Teleknosis' which can harness the power and can only be generated by the Telepaths' 'high vibration-al mutts' which are infused into their heart, and when the low vibration-al and un-reactive 'Neutrinos' from black holes are harnessed by the Teleports and passed through 'Teleknosis' they become highly reactive with the Xeone's atoms causing them to split open a space-time and light bending portal. The infected residents are injected with 'Memoria - beta-blockers', which erases the memories of their entire existence from Xeone. They are taken into the individual cockpit case, placed onto the passage track of the Teleknosis portal machine and are sent out creating a wormhole to another unknown destination.

It is believed that the ones, who are transported from Xeone to different destinations, one of them which is the nearest destination through the Black Hole, can be Earth. It can be postulated that what if the people who are reported to have no trace of their memory from where they have been rescued may have been a living resident of Xeone. Not only limited to that, if a full scientific cum medical examination takes place it will be observed the difference in the DNA modelling, along with the frequency in which they vibrate in this world is very different from the rest of the residing population.

But these are only mere postulates.

Concluding

Earth

I. If such institution of Psychic Establishment exists in our World, things would be as similar as in Xeone, the workload will ease and everyone will be placed in each sector of work according to their Psychic abilities, this will also open multiple assumptions, what if a systemic caste-ism exist due to the ascribed nature of their birth into a particular hold of power. The laws of Earth will also alternate itself which will cycle itself around the protection of rights of the people under their power.

There might be jurisdiction to each different psychic power holding sects of the society. There might be again the unequal distribution of respect and existence which will be judged how useful their Psychic ability is for the running of the Nation. Discrimination might exist on the supremacy of their worth under their power. Certain sects could only come to power and rest will cease to be mundane day to day chores.

On the other hand, if the technology is advanced by the nature of psychic powers the face of techs will be very advanced and different from what we have now. Teleporting from one distance to others might be one step away. A lot of man-labour might be broken down to only psychic labour and harnessing it using different technological methods. If Psychic powers are heightened with advanced technology, they might be also able to communicate with the souls of the dead from different realms.

II. If such institutions thrive on Earth where there is the invention of 'Teleknosis' and capital punishment means teleporting humans to different dimensions or universes, it can trigger a sequence of consequences:

a) If such invention takes place that means the potential technological updates are highly advanced.

b) Any person suffering from chronic, transmitted diseases rather than being treated patiently will be eliminated from the Earth to unknown dimensions.

c) Anybody, if framed precisely, could be (having personal grudges) taken advantage of by the system and eliminate them from the mere existence of Earth.

d) The Government could use this as a system of oppression towards the minority people. Further, it will be easy for the Government to eliminate the whole existence of any person who appears as a threat towards them.

e) It can be used as a means of Ethnic Cleansing, making an entire community go extinct.

d) It might lead to an uprising of Authoritarianship among the power holders of the world.

4

BE CAREFUL WHAT YOU WISH FOR

BY PRATHIBHA SRINIVASAN

S he hurried towards the place where she was meeting up with her friends and increased her pace as the sky darkened above her. She lamented the fact that it would start to rain today of all days, her car had gone for service and she had foregone the public transport in favour of walking. She had thought that walking would be a good way to let off steam, except now she felt that it was adding on to her anger.

"I wish I could kill that stupid oaf and the good for nothing manager. They're seriously testing my patience", she muttered to herself as she continued to hasten her steps.

Just as it looked like she was bound to get drenched in the rain, she finally reached the restaurant where she was meeting up with her friends. She swept into the building right as the sky gave way to the first drops of what would turn out to be a record-breaking rainstorm. She glanced at the crowd and was searching for the familiar faces of her friends when one of them caught sight of her and waved towards her, signaling that she should come on over to where they were seated. She made her way past the densely packed bodies as she once again cursed herself for living in such a crowded city. It seemed that even the comforting sight of her friend's face wasn't doing anything to soothe her mind. She finally reached them and took a note of everyone present. "Oh joy, I'm the only one who has arrived late!" she thought to herself bitterly as she took the seat that was offered to her. After she was seated, she looked up to see that all her friends appeared to be tensed about something. Thinking that their mood was somehow related to her tardiness she hastened to explain when her friend beat her to it and mentioned that they were all discussing their bad days, which was the reason for their collective sour mood.

"So, what happened to you all?" She asked the friend sitting beside her.

"We have all had really bad days at work today, especially Aryan. Aryan had a meeting with his boss today, he thought they were going to discuss his promotion but instead they fired him."

"What? Why?" She turned towards Aryan, who was sitting dejectedly and playing around with his drink. She noticed that Aryan wasn't looking at anyone, it looked like he was trying to control his emotions. She placed her hand on top of his and asked him what happened. Aryan looked up at her and shrugged, he said,

"The manager wanted to hire his wife's brother for my position. He couldn't recommend his brother-in-law as long as I was working there. He tried to make it look like I was incompetent, that anyone can do this job better than me. When it didn't work, he started making up stories about me and today he somehow showed "proof" that I was working against the company and so they decided to fire me."

She sat there looking stunned as she listened to her friend's story, "How can they do that?" she asked but no one had an answer to her question. She looked around the table as each of her friends started pouring out their tales of misery. She thought she could relax and wind-down after the awful day that she had but it didn't look like that was going to be possible. With every new story that was told, she could feel her rage and anxiety increasing, not at her friends but at the situation and the people that had led them to this state.

After her friends had finished recounting their woes, they all looked at her expectantly. They thought that she might have a nice fun story to light up their day. She was usually the one they would all go to when they had a bad day as she always had a repertoire of funny stories that would make them laugh till their sides ached, her wit was legendary in their small group. Unfortunately for her friends today was not that day, she had her own problems to spout out and a mood that was growing increasingly dark. She turned towards her friends and started recounting the day's events that caused her bad mood.

Her car had refused to start in the morning, and she had to catch a taxi to reach her office. She was a whole half hour late and was called into her lecherous manager's cabin, he had both reprimanded and tried to misbehave with her, but she managed to escape from his clutches. Her teammate was inept at his work and had managed to screw up their project and had caused her to receive the flak for it from their boss. Her manager and the oaf that she called a teammate continued to make her day get worse and worse until she was so angry, she could burst.

When she finally left the office, she felt like she could murder someone, specifically the two who were the cause of her misery. She then had to walk for almost an hour to reach the restaurant and almost got caught in a rainstorm for her efforts. After she finished telling her story, she looked around the table, all of her friends were silent. No one tried to speak up, everyone was wallowing in their misery with no signs of breaking out of it. When the silence was starting to become too deafening Aryan-who until then was a silent spectator, spoke up.

"You've all read the Strange case of Dr. Jekyll and Mr. Hyde, right? Sometimes I wish we lived in a world where that is possible. Imagine if we could channel our anger, our vices and all other problems into a likeness of us, wouldn't that be a problem solver?" He looked over at the group after his unexpected outburst, all his friends were gaping at him as if he had finally lost the plot.

"Come on guys, don't tell me that you've never thought of something like that? Don't you feel that you want to act upon your feelings without fearing any consequences?" Seeing that his friends were still unconvinced he tried to change their minds.

"Just humour me guys, can we just talk and fantasize about this? It's not like it's ever going to become a reality. I just want to let off steam and cheer us all up, help me out here." He stated the last line looking at her. She immediately caught onto what Aryan was trying to do. She said, "I agree with Aryan, let's create our version of Dr. Jekyll and Mr. Hyde, let's imagine an alternate planet where we can make our own rules. Let your creativity flow people!"

Slowly her friends started getting into that idea. They ordered drinks for their table and made it into a drinking game. They would take a sip of the drink and tell the others what they would make their alter ego do at an alternate planet in their alternate reality. There were a lot of creative answers and some very graphic ones too, but it helped the friends to let loose and they were all laughing by the time half the table was done. This went on for a long while until it was time for the restaurant to close for the night.

They all left in better spirits than they were in when they came to the restaurant. She was waiting outside for Aryan, he was going to drop her at her home seeing as the rain was still pouring heavily. After he dropped her off at her place, she went inside and changed into her nightwear. She always read a book before sleeping, that night she decided to reread Dr. Jekyll and Mr. Hyde as their dinner conversation was still fresh in her mind.

She could not manage to read more than ten pages and after reading the same line for what felt like the twentieth time, she decided that it was time to call it a night. She placed the book on her nightstand and switched off the lamp and prepared to sleep. Before sleep could fully occupy her, she let her mind wander over that day's events and the discussion with her friends. She was still annoyed when she thought about her manager and teammate. She wished that the alternate reality that they had envisioned in depth would finally become her reality just as her consciousness waned and she drifted off into deep sleep.

She woke up the next day, bright-eyed and refreshed. Today was the weekend and she had no work to do or office to go to. She was looking forward to the start of the new day, surprisingly buoyant in mood. She took a nice leisurely bath and made herself a strong, hot cup of coffee that she promptly carried with her to the balcony as she enjoyed the view before her while taking a slow sip of the comforting beverage in her hand. So lost in her thoughts was she, that she did not notice nor read the newspaper headlines as she carried it inside. It was not until late afternoon when she switched on the TV did she get an inkling as to how things had turned very, very bad in her world.

She turned on the news as she got ready to prepare her lunch.

Just as she was entering the kitchen an announcement from the TV caught her attention. She went into the hall, where the TV was kept, right as her friend Aryan appeared on the screen. Her hand flew to her mouth in shock as she read the news headlines shown on the screen. Aryan had been arrested for killing his office manager, the very same person who had falsely accused him to get him fired from his job.

"How can this be possible? No, this is a mistake." She said to herself as she continued looking at the TV in disbelief. She searched for her phone, she wanted to call her friends and find out if it was the truth or if her mind was playing tricks on her. She could not find her phone fast enough; she had silenced it last night and threw it onto a chair that was piled with clothes. After she dug her phone out from underneath the mound of clothes, she switched it on and found that she had more than a hundred missed calls from all her friends.

Her heart racing, she dialled Aryan's number and the call got picked up within the first ring. Aryan's sister answered his phone and tearfully explained that the police had entered their home in the early hours of the morning, saying that he was under arrest for the murder of his manager. His sister told her that Aryan could not have committed the murder as he came home immediately after meeting his friends. But the police told them that they had CCTV evidence which proved that Aryan was the person who committed the crime.

She cut the call after placating Aryan's sister and promising her that she and their friends would do everything in their power to prove that Aryan was innocent, and this was all a huge mistake. She then threw herself down into the nearest chair and dropped her head into her hand, attempting to clear her mind.

She went over the happenings of the previous day and was becoming more and more sure that there had been a mistake.

She called all her friends, and they were all equally shocked as she was. They decided to go to the police station and recount everything that had happened the previous day, to try and prove that Aryan was innocent.

She walked towards her room to get changed before she left. As she entered the room, she felt that there was something wrong. She felt a movement near the balcony door and turned and almost fainted. Standing at the entrance to the balcony was her doppelganger. She thought that her mind was playing tricks on her again. Her doppelganger walked towards her and said, "This is not a work of your imagination, I am real, and I am standing right in front of you." She managed to stutter out, "How?" "Have you ever heard of the phrase, be careful what you wish for?" Her doppelganger answered her as she strode over to her dresser and sat upon it, smirking darkly at her.

She picked up a picture frame from the dresser and traced over the people in the photo as she continued with her explanation, "Don't you remember wishing for an alternate universe where you can channel your vices into an alter ego and have them do all your dirty work in your stead." She raised an eyebrow at her mockingly, "Consider that your wish has been granted."

"But I don't understand! This can't be real; I must be dreaming. I should wake up soon!" The original one continued to babble to herself in growing horror, refusing to believe everything that had happened that day as the truth.

The doppelganger turned towards her and said, "Continue to live in your castle of dreams by all means, I have an important work to attend to or should I say two important works." There was a dark inflexion in her voice as she said that last bit.

The woman looked up into her doppelganger's face and

asked her with palpable fear in her voice, "What are you talking about, what important job?"

The doppelganger gave a sarcastic laugh dripping with dark glee as she said, "Don't you remember wanting to squeeze the life out of your manager and that idiot you call a teammate?"

"No, no this cannot be real. No, this has got to be a nightmare. No, you cannot do that. Please don't do that. Please go away and leave me alone!" She continued to scream at her doppelganger. She had trouble understanding everything that was going on in front of her.

"Oh! But you see, I cannot do that. You wished me into existence, but you have no say in my actions. So, sit back and enjoy as I go and do the things that you're too much of a coward to do." So saying, with a half-smirk etched on her face, the doppelganger jumped out of the balcony and gave her a mocking wave.

She continued to stare at the balcony, the place from which her doppelganger had vanished out of sight. She could not comprehend what was happening and started to feel that her sanity was slipping away from her. She could feel her grip on her consciousness slowly leaving her. As she was teetering over the edge between consciousness and unconsciousness one sentence kept playing around in her head, getting louder by the minute.

It was, "What have we done?"

5

THE DRAIN

BY SHUBHA PAI

"Oh C'mon Mom! It's Sunday for God's sake. I have other plans" complained Adhir. "Oh, I'm so sorry for interrupting your comics reading time with important works like fixing the drain." said Mom sarcastically. Adhir grunted and went to his room and did the most typical teenager thing – slam the door. Mom smiled and shook her head. Adhir picked up the 'Crisis on Earth Three' comic and started reading it when he heard his mom say, "Well, I'm pretty sure Batman listens to his mother." Adhir rolled his eyes and came out of his room.

"Batman's parents are dead." he exclaimed. Mom rolled her eyes and said, "Okay. If not Batman, Spider-Man." Adhir picked up the washed dishes and started wiping them dry. "Spider-man is Marvel, Batman is DC." he said calmly. Mom shrugged and said, "Same thing" Adhir let out a deep breath and said softly, "DC is rawer, it's darker and cooler." "You know what else is dark and cool? The drain! Just fix it before I get back from the mall." ordered Mom and left.

Adhir threw his hands up in the air and went to get the tools to fix the kitchen drain. He sat down near the drain and pulled out the pipe to check the blockage. A rumbling sound came from the drain. Adhir was surprised and scared at the same time. Is that a rat? he thought. He decided to look inside the drain with all the courage he had. He bent over the drain and tried to get a look when he fell inside the drain. Adhir was confused. He didn't know how it was possible, but he knew for a fact that he was inside his 2- inch diameter drain. The next thing he knew he was sliding down, what he imagined to be, a slide with darkness all around. He landed on the ground with a thud. When he opened his eyes, he was in a park. People around him were staring at him and few girls were winking at him. Adhir got up with a start and started wondering where he was.

He started walking in some direction trying to find someone he could talk to. As he started walking, he saw a bunch of girls standing near motorbikes. He contemplated asking them help as he didn't know how they would react to a stranger of the opposite sex approaching them and didn't want to take that risk. He went past them when he heard them catcalling. "Hey, sexy!" called out one. "Are you lost, baby boy?", asked another. "At least give me your number!" teased one and they collectively laughed.

Adhir was baffled. Are they eve-teasing me? I mean this is like adam-teasing, he thought. He ran as fast as he could and heard them cursing behind him. There were older men and women strolling on the roads which was surprising because the sky was pitch dark as if it were midnight. There were young men walking in boxers. Adhir heard a few older men grumbling behind him. "Oh God. Boys these days wear such short clothes. When we were young our fathers used to get us grounded if we did not tuck in our shirts and boys these days are roaming shamelessly." ranted an old man. "Exactly!", added another. "That too, they walk in front of the girls to provoke them and then put harassment cases on our daughters." The former oldie said, "Tell me about it. They think they can do anything in the name of menism."

Adhir felt he would lose his mind with all this confusion. Am I dreaming? Why are things in reverse here? he thought. He was walking lost in his thoughts when he was stopped. He looked up to see the same girl gang who were Eve -tea – uh, Adam-teasing him earlier. "Why did you run away from us, hottie?" asked one of them with weird lust in her eyes. Adhir traced back a few steps and started to run when one of the girls held his hand with great strength. Oh God, no, he thought. "Leave him alone" thundered a girl's voice.

Adhir and the girl gang looked from where the voice came. A girl, about Adhir's age, was standing confidently with a hockey stick in her hand. The girl holding Adhir's hand cursed under her breath and let his hand go. Adhir did not move as he was busy looking at the girl who saved him. I have seen her somewhere, he thought. The girl gang ran away as Adhir's saviour came towards him. "Are you okay?" she asked. "Yes, thank you." said Adhir. "Are you new here? I've never seen you around." she said. "That's exactly what I'm trying to figure out. But firstly, have we met before? You look very familiar." Adhir said hesitantly. "I was wondering the same thing! My name is Ridha, by the way." exclaimed the girl and smiled as she extended her hand. "Hi Ridha. I'm Adhir.", said Adhir shaking her hand.

Ridha laughed and said, "Do you realise your name is just the other way round of my name? R- I- D-H-A and A- D-H-I-R. "Adhir's eyes went wide as he realised where he had seen Ridha before. "You – you. are me!" stammered Adhir. Ridha looked confused. "Uh. I'm who?" she asked. Adhir started strolling back and forth with his head in his hands. "Oh god. Oh god. How can this be? How could you be me? Where am I?" he kept talking to himself. "Um maybe you're just tired. You need to take rest. I don't think you ate anything. Let's first go and have dinner. It's already 4 am." suggested Ridha.

Adhir cut her short, "Wait... wait. It is 4 am in the morning? How come everyone is going for a walk this early? When do they sleep?" Ridha looked at him bewildered and said, "At 8 am, silly." Adhir was shocked. "They sleep at 8 am and wake up at?". Ridha said, "Well, it depends on people. I like to wake up early for college. So, I wake up at 11pm." Adhir felt like his head is going to explode. "You people sleep the whole day?", he managed to ask. Ridha laughed and said, "That's what the day is for! You sleep in the day and work at night." "Which planet are you from?", she added sarcastically. "Earth" said Adhir in a reflex.

Ridha stopped laughing. "Did you just say you're from Earth?" she asked. Adhir feared what's coming next. "Don't tell me this is not Earth, please.", he cried. Ridha was silent. Then she spoke suddenly as though she understood the whole thing. "Oh my god! This is like the Reverse flash paradox! You're from another planet that's the opposite of ours!" she shouted with excitement. Adhir asked, "You mean like the flashpoint paradox?" Ridha said, "Um yeah. I am guessing Flash is like a superhero in the comics of your world. Welcome to Thrae, our planet." Adhir could not take it anymore, he fainted.

When he woke up, he was in a room that looked like his, but not his. Probably Ridha's, he thought. "Hey! You woke up." said Ridha. She handed him a cool drink. "Drink this. You will feel better.", she advised. Adhir shook his head and chuckled. Cool drink instead of Coffee, he thought. "No thank you. I feel better now.", he said. He looked around the room. There were many posters of Thanos, Red-Skull, Dormamu and other Marvel villains along with Hitler, Joseph Stalin and Genghis

Khan. "Woah. You are hard-core. Are you like the evil version of me?", asked Adhir half- smiling and half – genuinely scared. Ridha laughed and asked, "Why do you ask that?" Adhir said hesitantly, "Well, you have posters of all these villains and evil dictator-" Ridha interrupted, "WHAT?! Adolf, Joseph and Khan are evil in your world? They are peace lovers and one of the kindest people in history for us. You called the other villains, does that mean the Avengers are heroes for you people?" Adhir laughed and said, "Yeah. Looks like we are not very alike, though. You are a Marvel fan and I'm a DC fan." Ridha smiled and said, "Well, I find Batman, Superman and all very, I don't know, I don't want to hurt any sentiments here." Both laughed understandingly. Ridha said, "It's just that I like Marvel more because it's rawer. You know it's darker and –" "Cooler", Adhir completed the sentence with disbelief. Ridha's jaw dropped.

"Looks like this Earth thing is really a complete opposite of our planet. Does that mean you don't have Matriarchy in your world?" Ridha asked. Adhir shook his head and said, "We have patriarchy. You saw the way I got into trouble this morning? That is what women face back in my world. We have a movement called feminism." Ridha smirked, "Feminism, sounds weird. Looks like there's no equality and justice in any world." Adhir smiled sadly.

"Oh! Do you have a pet?", Ridha changed the topic. Adhir said, "Yes, a dog. Her name is Sandy." Ridha looked at Adhir wide – eyed. "You people have dogs as your pets? Wow. You are pretty brave." said Ridha. Adhir felt good for the first time. Maybe they have rats or frogs as pets, he thought. "Oh, meet my pet, Boxer.", said Ridha as she called out for Boxer. A lion twice as big as Adhir came into the room with an excitement that could kill both. Adhir became speechless, he knew he could listen to his heart pounding inside his chest. "He is very friendly. Come and tell him hi, Boxer.", said Ridha. "I don't think that's necessary- "before Adhir could complete his sentence, the golden furred beast leapt on him and started licking him.

Adhir passed out and the last thing he could remember was Boxer's heavy paw on his chest. Adhir woke up with a start as Sandy was licking his face. Adhir looked around, he was back in his room. Was that all a dream? he thought. Sandy was wagging her tail. Adhir smiled and patted her. He looked at his phone. It was 7 am in the morning. He smiled again thinking about the sleep cycle in his dream. Was that really a dream? he thought.

"Adhir! Are you up?", called out mom. Adhir woke up with a weird pain in his chest. Is this because of – no, no. It is just in my head, he thought. Mom entered the room and asked, "Which world are you in?" "Huh? Oh. Yeah, I'm coming.", said Adhir. "Are you okay? You look lost.", asked Mom with concern. Adhir smiled and said, "I'm okay, Ma. Just had a weird dream." Mom said, "Okay. Come soon. I know it's Sunday, but you have a lot of work to do. Remember there's a drain you need to fix?" Adhir became stiff. That means the whole parallel universe episode never happened, he thought. He was happy and sad. He really wanted his meeting with Ridha to be true, but he also didn't want to put his head in the Lion's mouth, quite literally.

Adhir freshened up and was about to go for breakfast when he paused. He looked at the Justice League poster in his room and smiled. He kissed the poster and whispered, "You people are the best." He was having his breakfast when Mom said, "Please make sure you fix the drain before I come from the mall. You can read your comics later." Adhir got the tools and was ready to fix the drain. Just before checking the drain, he paused.

He shook his head and started checking for the blockage. He removed the pipe slowly and peeped inside to check what was blocking the water. He tried to clear it with the drain plunger, but it was still blocked. He put his hand inside the drain and removed the dirt that was causing the blockage. Adhir looked at it and fell back. There lay in front of him, a ball of lion fur.

6

UTOPIA

BY ADITHYA AJ

Prologue

Perhaps there never was enough time for any of us", Ema confessed to herself, speeding on that forsaken road, mother's poem pacing in her mind:

> *'Stars are souls, less and more*
>
> *Mates in soul, mine & yours, a lore*
>
> *Not realer than all the lives we stole.*
>
> *And the first dawn shall arrive to show*
>
> *That stars shall reap all they were swore'*

What she meant, more apparent now, with each echo, she ran on, coughing… choking on nothing except these words that she barely spit out in a whisper to only the darkness that had mere minutes to become her home; forever. A single star feebly twinkling, barely breathing, bore witness as she ran through the gates, besides the *inhuman* silence. Breaking in through the window, she found **Ios** and unchained him, "Run boy, run away into this new world cleansed of humans." Now she had nothing left to do… *nothing* at all. So, she sat on the steps of her mansion, staring at the lonely star twinkle fainter every moment, waiting for it to die. Tears flooded her cheeks, but it was not sorrow and neither was it pain, it was something else… something very numb inside her. Memories flashed against the darkest sky she'd ever seen, and she started reminiscing, *everything*, her childhood… the dream… the nightmare, *everything* played in slow motion, stretching seconds into ages, as she stared at the dying star, knowing full well the star's death would kill her too.

Emergence

'It almost feels like a different life… even a different reality', Ema thought, as blurry recollections rushed her. 'Even my name feels like someone else's… **Ema Erèinred**, Rescues Division with PETA, for the country of **Urapsid**, saving animals from mankind, with all heart, to end animal slavery and to work for a world where animal rights and human rights meant equal rights. The starkest memory I have now, of committing to this cause is when father took us picnicking and I found a friend in this beautiful, lonely fawn in that meadow. Eyes as big as lucky 8 balls, it instantly trusted me so much that it came to me and we played, rolling in the grass together, as my little sister **Tlunèp,** kept watching from afar, loathingly. The fawn and I played for so long that we both fell asleep, exhausted. When I awoke, it was gone, and I got sad but *Tlunèp* kept me distracted. It was only when we were about to leave and I went to the pond to wash up that I found the fawn's severed head, bobbing in it and only then did I realize what we had for lunch. I screamed so furiously that I fainted'.

'There was no turning back from that moment. It opened me up to what monsters we were, and I went on to save hundreds of thousands of animals, world over and yet, for every life that we rescued, hundred others were lost. What a pity! It boiled my blood to see blunt human cruelty. My soul hurt every time I read a story about an elephant butchered for ivory or of some tannery. The one regret that I will not be carrying to my grave though, is that little *Tlunėp* is now a vegetarian. The day I knew she realized, after so many years from the day that I realized that killing animals was plainly wrong... that was the inception of all this... all this death. Do I regret it? I'm not sure'.

Prelude

'That fateful day, my team was scheduled to visit the Rottnest archipelago to survey the dwindling population of native Quokkas. Our data showed that even with predatory species like foxes and cats appearing, the population decline was far too great, and we had to investigate. I took *Tlunėp* along, as this was a low-risk mission, and the gentle quokkas might spark something in her'.

"I'm glad you brought me" *Tlunėp* exclaimed, "these little guys are cute!" I left her to spend some time with the animals, in a local rescue shelter and moved on with the fieldwork, tagging and tracking some selective specimens. We did find some carcasses of quokkas consistent with the feeding pattern of cats but nothing that would account for the rapid plunge in their numbers. After the day's work, the team was moving out, when *Tlunėp* came to me, asking to stay back for the night and spend another day with the animals. Torn between my desperation for a chance like this to finally change her and my team's schedule to arrive at the base, I chose both. I asked the team to move on without us and that I will connect with them remotely during the following day's briefing.'

'We spent the night on the shore listening to whales sing in the distance, far from where most humans can touch them.' "You know what makes me love the oceans so much?" I asked her rhetorically, "it's because I know that at least here, most beings are safe from human predators." I thought *Tlunêp* looked at me like she was going to tell me to not give her another lecture but what she said was nothing I would have expected her to say. "I understand you; I feel your compassion for animals. It is so powerful that just watching you can inspire many of us; even someone like me". To say the least, I thought I was dreaming but what she said next brought tears to my eyes: "I have been trying for over a year now, to quit meat, unsuccessfully. It is all you, you inspired me to try. The way you toil, risk and dedicate your whole life to saving them moved me and I wanted to be one less person you must go through to get to your dream. And I honestly believe you will get there someday, and I will be there proudly, watching as someone who's been changed by you."

'I was left speechless. She said what she said as if she did not expect me to respond to it. Like she knew how it would affect me and she understood. I could feel that when she put her arm around me, leaning her head on my shoulder as we saw the full moon shimmer on the ocean, the silence only broken by the waves breaking on some rocks, somewhere'.

'It was then that we heard it, the shrill of a woman, not far from us, as if something were attacking her, running towards us! We could hear the undergrowth getting pounded under her feet through the woods directly behind our cabin and she was running fast. Then there was another cry for help, and we were too scared to move. Our local contact had gone into town on some errand and wasn't going to return for at least another hour. We had to do something. We both knew we had the same thing on our minds when we looked at each other and ran to grab my flare, a torch and a kitchen knife from the cabin and we ran toward the echoes of these footsteps that we were going to meet head on, if we kept our course. But about a few yards away, we couldn't hear their footfalls anymore. At first, I thought it was my panting and my pounding heart that impaired my hearing when we stopped to listen but even Tlunèp couldn't hear a thing! All was quiet again, as if it was all a prank and Tlunèp screamed "Who's there?" in her coarse, almost male voice so loud that it echoed for seconds and then we heard the footsteps retracting, away from us. We couldn't make out the number of people running but we then heard muffled cries and moaning about just a few meters to our right. When we reached the spot, our very souls left our bodies.'

Inception

'It started raining and the blood-soaked dead leaves appeared blacker than the starry night itself, in the bright moon light that seeped in through the double canopy of treetops and storm clouds. But even by that faint light, there was no mistaking... what we saw was death itself. Strewn all around the place were dead cats as black as the blood that oozed from their wounds and I broke down into tears. I couldn't see clearly in the rain and my tears were not helping either, as I started searching for any cats that were still alive and could be helped to survive this massacre. But Tlunèp found where the moans were coming from. Having found none of the felines alive, I strode over to her side, sitting down heartbroken, anguish crushing my gut and anger beyond any I had ever felt. Such beautiful creatures! So *many* of them... and for what? **Nothing.** Absolutely nothing. I punched the ground with my fist not knowing if it was mud or stone and let out a scream that scared even Tlunèp.

She shook me to my senses saying, "The cats may be dead, but we might still be able to save her."

'It was then that she spoke "...survive... erut..." we couldn't hear her, she lost so much blood that she could barely speak. So I leant in and Tlunèp tried to get up saying she would call emergency services, but the old woman pulled her close and tried to speak again "I won't survive this, I can feel it. Please stay here... don't leave me." We looked at her and realized she was right.

With great effort, she continued speaking, "I am **Erutan** and I'm 400 years old, so your medicine won't work on me, anyway..."

"...also, I'm a witch."

At this point us sisters looked at each other and couldn't decide if she was babbling out of fear, with oxygen supply depleted from her brain or if she was telling the truth because now that she mentioned it, she sure looked like one. "If you're a witch, why won't you heal yourself", mocked Tlunèp, in an obvious attempt to keep her awake. "It doesn't work that way, child", said the woman, "witchcraft isn't magic, there are only a few things we misunderstood witches can do."

"Misunderstood how?" Tlunèp jutted.

"We do not harm people like you fear we do, we just perform what is necessary to maintain the balance but for the past few centuries, it hasn't been working. We had all been hunted down and I'm probably the last one alive" she murmured, tears filling her eyes for the first time.

"Who tried to kill you?" I asked her.

"It does not matter, some commoners, scared of my kind. That does not matter now, *nothing* does. All my babies, my cats are murdered... *MURDERED!*" she shrieked devilishly, and malice sprouted on her face now, like an eclipse over the moon, as she continued "But now, with my last breath, I shall lay a curse on all those who hurt my babies! They shall suffer the same fate as we do, for having killed these pure, innocents in cowardice... **they shall all *pay!*"**

"But if you truly want to avenge the murders of innocent beasts, why not avenge all beasts? Why not curse all those who'll ever hurt any animal?" I asked her, remembering a curse from a bedtime story that mom used to read to me, about an alternate reality where anyone who hurts an animal is killed in the same fashion that they kill the animal; because I knew that this old hag was just out of her mind in her final moments and I was just trying to indulge her.

"Ah... so you've heard of the world of ***Etsixe?***" she asked, half surprised.

"Yeah... yeah... we've all heard that fairytale" I yawned.

"**Fool!** *Etsixe* is no myth! And you shall bear witness soon" barked the self-proclaimed witch, as if she forgot she was dying'.

'Then she yelled, her fists clenched over her walking stick "htaed nika eb tlaed ot lla ohw gnirb htaed ot stsaeb " and then turned to us "the curse's been laid, anyone who harms an animal from the moment my kitties were harmed, shall die. You've been warned!" as if she'd just cast a powerful spell.

"Lady, you made no sense!" pointed Tlunèp but the witch cackled *"mirror worlds need mirrored words to be mirrored"* and burst into a wild laughter, as if she'd gone mad in her final moments. I tried to ring up the emergency services earlier, but my phone was soaked and so was Tlunèp's. She was dead before we could do anything else, her final laughter etched onto her face eternally'.

Exists

'Morning brought devastating news as we finally got done with our statements with the police. The ship that was carrying our crew hit a whale and sank to the bottom of the ocean, *along with the dead whale.* I was still too sleepless and fatigued from last night to have absorbed this fresh impact and yet it hit like a boulder. Then we overheard the comms on the cops report a wet-market turning into a whole slaughterhouse, as every last monger died this *dawn,* from what appeared to be an armed strike on the market with swords and katanas but no traces of the killers were to be found"

Tlunèp and I looked at each other unable to believe what we were hearing but we were still unconvinced.

Unconnected deaths started happening all over the world and we never connected the dots until... tragedy struck at our very home. When we arrived, we found father dead in the kitchen, the duck that he'd killed still in his hand and we knew. Without doubt, without even looking at each other... *we just knew.* The realms of **Etsixe** not only existed but had now merged with our own and laws of physics and nature have all been blended between the two realms!

The world was ending'.

'It was then that it struck me, in dad's funeral. I ran to mom, who was a very practical woman, an astrophysicist and a poetess who married dad just because he could fund all her research and why dad married her, we never knew. I ran to her and asked her to tell me of *Etsixe.* She was perplexed at the timing of my question but knowing I wouldn't do anything lightly, she budged: "you know how animals are sacred and were as gods in the land of *Etsixe...*"

"Yes, mom... I know that animal killers died and all, but was there anything to the story that you didn't tell us?" I begged impatiently.

"It's funny you should mention that, because I was thinking about the same thing when we found a bunch of actual stars were missing. At first, we thought it was a mistake but all readings from around the world read the same! So, we figured we must be missing something and were firing up the ISS to take charge of the investigation because obviously, stars don't just disappear! Then I heard of your father's death and left everything to get here but what bears a striking resemblance to the legend of *Etsixe* is that in the original text of the tale, before it was modified to be a children's book, every soul of every man was entangled with a star and if one died, the other died too. And I wrote a nice little poem of it too!"

'That was a week ago, and she's dead now too. We had to do something to undo the curse. We reached out to multiple authorities of many lands, using father's money and reach in government but none believed us, even with all that is going on, because there were so many hoax calls that no one could tell what's real anymore. We searched for clues in the witch's last resort, but none turned up'.

'The world keeled over, normalcy died, millions perished each day, and the human race was going extinct. Bodies strewn across countries, most of the dead still rotting in their homes. It had now been a fortnight since the witch died knowing there was no one left to undo her curse. Not just those who slaughtered or caged animals but those who affected deaths of animals indirectly with plastics in the ocean or contributed to global warming or even those who used insecticides were all dying, and stars kept dropping from the sky as if autumn infected the heavens. The last of us, those who believed me at least, realized we couldn't do a thing to save ourselves. So, we started freeing pets from their cages, with the owners dead and no one to feed them'.

'That was until yesterday, when I remembered there was no one to free my father's dog Ios too, and I came over to free him. And a single star remains now, as I sit on these steps... so that means Tlunèp's dead somewhere too, trying to rescue someone's pet. I will be gone too now, it's just a matter of minutes... I can feel my body going numb but...

Where's it?

It's *nowhere...*

The last star... it's gone... I'm sure, there's not a cloud in the skies. But then... *How am I alive*?

Am I already dead?'

The Dawn

'Light's pouring in like wax from a cheap candle and I'm still not sure if I'm alive but then I am! I'm sure I am alive because Ios is licking me and I can feel it on my fingers. But how am I still alive when the star entangled with my soul has died?

How?

Why?

I pondered the reason for my survival, laden with the assumed guilt of *entire* humanity's death, staring helplessly into the brightening horizon for an hour now, without success but...

I see it now!

Is that it? Is it that simple?

Is the sun really my answer?

But... why?'

7

WHAT'S MY PURPOSE?

BY SHIVANGI GUPTA

Allie, you haven't done anything right the past couple of days. I think it's in everyone's best interest that you take some time off", says Mr. Martinez, the boss, while distastefully looking towards Allie. As much as it stung her to hear that, she knew, he was right. She'd been a wreck lately. But how could she not, after everything that had happened.

One moment you think you have it all figured out, but in the next it so happens that there was that one thing you left unaccounted in your wonderful plan, assuming it would never come to that, and well, it does.

A week ago, she was a regular girl in her 20s, with a happy family, a decent job, wonderful friends, and a caring boyfriend. It was a good life, and she was grateful for it. But today, she wasn't just unemployed, she was about to lose the one woman who loved her unconditionally, who never failed to guide her and hold her when she was afraid, her support system, her mother. Her heart ached thinking of her mom undergoing treatment and lying unconscious for two days due to an accident. Her mother was so selfless, she didn't deserve any of this. Allie wasn't very close to her dad, they never opened up to each other, he was too busy with his work and they only spoke when necessary.

She sprinted to the washroom and stared at her reflection in the mirror, still had the same features but she couldn't recognize the person beneath it. It was as if her soul had been replaced with another, she had no idea who she was anymore, everything that was once clear was now a blur. She picked up her belongings and left the office. She knew she wasn't coming back anytime soon. Nothing made sense anymore. All she wanted was to be told that this was some sort of nightmare and she was going to wake up soon.

She had no idea why these awful things were happening to her, neither did she understand what the universe had in store by making her lose her mother this early. Everything happens for a reason, her mom used to say, if only something could justify this. If only she knew what to do or where to go from here. The uncertainty was appalling and if only there was some sort of guiding light.

It's crazy how life can turn upside down within a few seconds.

Allie wiped a tear with the hem of her left sleeve and decided to walk home. Her mind was racing with undesirable thoughts and she was paying no attention to the vehicles zooming past her. She'd barely slept a wink the last couple of days. Maybe it wasn't the best idea to walk, she wasn't in the right frame of mind for it. She crossed over to the other end of the street to catch a ride but as she did that, she stumbled over a rock and her head smashed against the edge of the curb and all she saw was the world going upside down before everything went black.

It'd been 4 hours. Or had it?

Allie regained consciousness and she was back in her room. She opened her eyes slowly and looked around, trying to adjust to the bright light. Her head was aching with such intensity. There was something off about the room she was in. The things were still hers', but they were arranged differently. She looked around trying to understand the surroundings and her eyes landed on a thick book by the bedside table that used to be on the left.

Allie reached for the book and stared at the cover, it had a hard wood covering with her name "Allison Campbell", engraved so deeply, as if the world had known of her existence for 1000s of years. She opened the book to a random page.

17th April 2018

I went to the Gildon tower and stopped Aiden from jumping. He hadn't fulfilled his purpose yet, and if he died before doing that, it would wreak havoc. According to the legends, all hell broke loose the last time someone did so. It broke my heart that we couldn't be with each other, but you don't choose who to fall for. Even if it's written by God himself.

"Oh my God! Aiden!", she exclaimed. Allie was in complete shock after reading that. She could not believe it. It was her handwriting, but she had no memory of writing that, much less the events occurring. Last she remembered; they were happy together. What was this book talking about?!

She flipped to another page.

31st December 2016

It was New Year's Eve. The fireworks were igniting the sky one after the other. It looked so beautiful that all I wanted was to freeze myself in that moment forever, away from the chaos that is my life. Every step I take has been so carefully written. I cannot break any rules. I cannot do what I wish to do, or I will disturb the balance. Hell, I am the balance. My life's purpose is to ensure that people around me fulfill theirs. It's too much, having to save the world almost every day. I wish to be liberated from this responsibility.

Allie's heart was racing while reading all of this. She could almost feel a panic attack coming. She had no idea what was happening. The book had similar entries almost every day. Either she was trying to keep something bad from happening or wishing she didn't have to. She flipped to yesterday's date.

29th September 2019

A huge fight broke out between residents of various streets. The essential supplies were running low and people living farther away from the shops were very furious. There were fires and several cases of vandalism. Things were getting out of control and its consequences would be dire. As the savior, I had to go and stop it. I had no choice. In the process of trying to do things for the greater good, I was attacked, and everything after that is blank.

She tried to recollect the incident, but suddenly had flashes of her mother being in a hospital bed, fighting for her life.

Allie freaked out, grabbed the book, and ran downstairs. Her father was walking by the porch, talking to someone on the phone. His hands were moving in an animated motion and it appeared as though he was in a heated conversation with someone. His demeanor was completely different from the kind of man she remembered him to be. He seemed more confident and authoritative as opposed to timid and secretive. She went over to him and asked for her mother; the only person Allie wanted to see right now and make sure was okay. Her dad looked at her with a puzzled expression and said, "Hey, honey, how are you feeling? And what did you just ask? Your mom has been gone for 22 years now. She died within a day of giving birth to you, remember? That was her life's purpose and she fulfilled it graciously."

Upon hearing that, Allie collapsed. Just when she thought that nothing could be worse than waking up in a world where people have their entire lives written beforehand, she found out that you die within 24 hours of fulfilling what you took birth for. And one of the victims of this ordeal was her own mother.

This was not what she'd asked for. What happens to her then, if she had to keep ensuring everyone lives to do what they were meant to? Does that mean she can't die, ever? How does this wretched thing even work? Several questions were racing in her head with nowhere to go to find the answers to them. She had to get out of there. The thought of being the reason for her mother's death was far greater than any kind of pain she had ever endured. The realities of this reality were too much to bear.

Before she could leave the house, though, her father stopped her and questioned, "Where are you going with your Lifeoure?"

The what? She wondered.

He pointed to the book in her hands.

Oh, so that's what this deranged thing is called. He continued, "It's dangerous out there. After what happened yesterday, several riots are happening. I just got off the phone with the mayor, he says they're trying to get things under control, but everyone needs to stay put."

What else happened yesterday? She thought.

"I can't lose you, Allie, the world can't. Not yet, anyway."

This piqued her curiosity instantly and she asked, "What do you mean, 'not yet'?"

"You're behaving very strangely, young lady. And honestly, I'm not sure why you keep asking these questions, you are fully aware of what you are. Are you alright? Tell me what's going on and let me help you", her father said with concern filled eyes.

Allie didn't know how to react to this, should she tell him everything that's been happening? Could she even trust this man who looked like her father but was nothing like him?

She was mentally battling these thoughts when an idea hit her. If she had a "Lifeoure", then he would too. And if she could somehow get her hands on that, it would answer some of her questions.

Allie looked around and saw a book similar to hers', lying on her father's desk. She then turned to him and said with a reassuring tone, "Hey, don't worry, I'm alright. Probably still recovering from the events of yesterday. I guess I just need to rest a little more and I'll be fine". He didn't look too convinced but decided to let it go.

After making sure he was out of sight, Allie sneaked into her father's room. She reached for the book and was surprised by its weight. It was quite heavy. She quickly ran to her room with the two books in hand and sat down to open the first page of her dad's Lifeoure.

Name: Thomas Campbell

Born: 24th July 1971

Purpose: To take down the longest running drug cartel in the country

Area of influence: Old Adamsborro

Premature death consequence: Drought for 17 years

Life Expectancy: 52 years [What?! He only had 4 more years to live?]

Love interest: Melinda Campbell

That was her mom, Melinda, a tear slipped down Allie's face thinking of her.

So, Thomas' purpose was to take down the biggest cartel and that's why he was involved with them. She then flipped to yesterday's date.

29th September 2019

Today was an important day at work. One of the biggest deals worth $900 million was supposed to close, and I had to ensure it didn't. I had made all the arrangements, and everything was going perfectly according to plan. And it did. Except when they found out that there was a mole who stopped the deal from happening.

I messed up and their wrath will take form in ugly ways. In the underworld, there's a punishment worse than death awaiting a betrayer. They will go to any lengths to find out who was behind it. They will not rest until they get to me. And I cannot leave without taking them down, for Allie.

Aghast. Horrified. Stunned. There weren't enough words to describe what Allie was feeling after reading that. She saw her dad in a new light, as brave. She saw him as someone who was fighting against all odds just to keep her safe, exactly what a father would do. She knew right away that she had to help him. She couldn't just let him do this all by himself, what kind of a daughter would that make her? But that would mean she would lose him sooner. Ugh! What was this life, she missed her old one. Things were so much easier. She had both her parents, at the very least.

Allie went down to speak to her dad. She sat across from him and he asked, "Hey, hon, any better?"

Allie said in a serious tone, "I'm fine. I want to help you".

Thomas developed a confused expression on his face. "What do you mean?"

"To achieve your purpose, I want to help you take them down".

"Well, I appreciate that, but you can't. This isn't like you. You know how it works around here. We need to focus on our respective roles, that's it, and everything will be fine".

"Except, everything is not fine. I don't like this life and maybe the only way of getting rid of it is to finish what I'm here for, and that means helping you.", Allie immediately reasoned.

"It's dangerous, Allie. Think about it before making any impulsive decisions".

"Oh, I'm aware of the danger. Look at what I've been doing my whole life here, I think I've become immune to any sort of threat that comes my way. I'm ready for this, dad".

Thomas sighed.

"Okay if we're going to do this, we'll need an army, and lucky for us, the government has our back.

Let me just inform them that Operation Gambit is on."

Thomas dropped a message to the mayor with the code word and by then Allie was all ears.

"Okay, the plan is really simple. Not easy, but simple. There are three main regions where they operate from. The first one is down Ambridge Street, the second is at the end of Mender Circle and the third and biggest one is inside the nuclear factory on the outskirts.

As they will be distracted trying to catch the mole, aka me, this will serve as the best opportunity to take them out. Remember, the element of surprise is all we've got. The other two regions are taken care of and everyone is ready in their positions, but Ambridge Street is a little tricky as it's very close to civilization. No civilians can get hurt in this process. This is where you come in. Your job is to ensure everyone within 2.5 miles radius is indoors no matter what."

Allie nodded and listened to everything very carefully.

"Everyone has already been alerted to stay indoors, making your task easier. The real danger is if one of their men see you. You need to hide; you need to take each step carefully. If they get even a little suspicious, this could be the end for all of us.

Meanwhile, we'd have surrounded them in all three spots and sealed their exit points thoroughly. The only thing remaining would be to burn it down with the inner circle members inside.

And after it's all done, we'll meet again to celebrate our victory.

So, are you ready?"

"Absolutely dad, let's get them". Allie exhaled with confidence.

She did exactly as she was told. She made no mistakes. She

used the element of surprise and took down as many of their men as she could.

After a while, she suddenly felt a heaviness around her. This meant that the operation had been successful. This meant that her father only had 24 hours remaining. Allie quickly went home to spend the last few hours with him, only to find it surrounded by police cars. She ran up to them and saw her father's still body. He had become a casualty in the process, he had sacrificed himself, he was the "Gambit".

She started yelling at no one in particular, "No, no, no! Please take me back! Please take me back! This can't be true." She couldn't stop crying. She didn't even get to say goodbye and now he was gone, she was all alone, again, and it hurt her so much that she suddenly went unconscious.

A couple of months later.

Allie woke up in a hospital room. It seemed familiar. She checked the date. 31st December 2019. It had been 3 whole months! The nurse came running in.

"Good! You're finally awake. Do you remember who you are?"

"Allison Campbell, daughter of Melinda and Thomas Campbell".

"That's perfect! Everyone was so worried you'd lose your memory. What is the last thing you recall?"

Everyone? Did she say, everyone?

"Who is everyone? And I remember being fired from my job after my mom met with an accident. Please tell me she's okay", Allie replies frantically.

"Your family and friends, darling. You're so lucky to have so many people that care about you. You hit your head while walking down the street and it caused a hemorrhage making you slip into a coma for 3 months. Honestly, it's a medical miracle that you recovered this quickly. And don't worry, your mom is just fine, she's on a wheelchair but will be on her feet in no time. Now, I need to inform everyone that you're up and arrange some medications, please rest".

Upon hearing that Allie wanted to jump with joy, not caring about all the wires and sedatives holding her down. She did the next best thing, she cried, she cried tears of joy. Everything was okay in this world. She didn't want anything to change. She cherished the freedom to make her own choices and decisions, good or bad, as long as they were hers. She loved that every little thing didn't have drastic consequences. She loved that new days meant new possibilities, and she could do anything she wanted. She loved that the world didn't rest on her shoulders and felt heavier every passing second. She loved that she could write her own story and boy, was she going to write it well. She loved that she had everyone she cared about and wasn't alone and that she didn't need to have it all figured out. She adored everything about this life and wouldn't have it any other way.

Allie spent that new years' eve with her loved ones, feeling happiness and content, her wishes had come true after all.

8

MAYBE SOMEWHERE ELSE

BY AKSHITHA GAJANAND

November 8th, 2019

Arshi slides into her shimmer dress, dancing to her playlist. She puts on her sparkling earrings, the one Abram gifted her. She selects the lipstick shade he likes and sends flying kisses to her reflection in the mirror. She doesn't need to apply blush as her cheeks are already red with excitement. As she takes a last look in the mirror, she lets her hair down, tucking it behind her ear, she smiles. She rushes to the dining room to place the chocolate cake she baked for him at the centre in a room full of balloons. She slows down the music when hears Abram's car. Arshi rushes to the door to find Abram in a suit, at the doorstep holding flowers, a tall guy, so charming that can make anyone fall in love with him with his one smile.

"Happy Anniversary. You're gorgeous." He says in his mellifluous voice handing her the flowers.

"Happy Anniversary to us." She blushes. It is their first anniversary.

She places the flowers in the vase and turns towards him. Abram walks close to her, touches her earring with his fingers, "You are adding beauty to these earrings." as they sparkle in his eyes. Arshi turns pink and warm.

"Come with me, I've to show you something." She holds his hand and walks him to the dining room.

"Did you jus... did you just do all this? You baked a cake?" He was impressed. He looks around and finds their pictures hanging down from the ceiling, "Wow! This is amazing, you're amazing."

"Wait, how did you reach the ceiling?" he smirked. He never leaves an opportunity to tease her height.

Arshi rolled her eyes, "I used a ladder."

Abram laughed, "Okay, let's cut the cake before it spoils." She punched him.

After the cake, he holds her hand and walks her to the car. He opens the door for her and makes her comfortable. Arshi turns around to place her jacket in the backseat and is surprised to see takeaways from their favourite restaurants.

"There's food for 20 of us. Why did you get so much food?" She was bemused.

"I didn't know what you're in the mood for, so I got them all."

"Where are we going? Roe Hills?" The place where they spent most of their time together. Her enthusiasm was unmatchable.

"There's no place better than Roe Hills." he laughed. Arshi brought Abram to the hills on their first date.

They reached a point on the hill which covers the whole city. They got on the roof of the car to watch the sunset. She loves watching the sunset and Abram loves the way her eyes twinkle when she talks about it.

"Our parents would get my brother and me to this place every weekend." She looked at him. "We used to run around to catch butterflies. We laughed, fought, ate and danced here, my brother and I would doze off by the time we reached home. I spent most of my childhood here, this place is so special to me." She added.

"Why did y'all stop coming?" he narrowed his eyebrows.

"We grew up. We still come here on New Year's." She looked at the sky.

Abram grew up in a different city and had a different life, far different than Arshi's. With his parents being busy with business and no one to nurture him, he was a spoiled kid. He always got into trouble as a child and grew up to be a heartbroken teenager. He turned into a taciturn man and raised his walls high which pushed everyone away until he met Arshi. She never gave up on him. She was all ears when he talked about his childhood. She pulled his leg and they giggled.

The sun slowly submerged into the buildings turning the purplish-pink sky to dark blue filled with stars. They witnessed the evening serenity. Abram jumps down and helps Arshi. He opened the deck lid of the car and pulled out a kong ming lantern and a marker.

Arshi gasped, "You don't believe in these!" She was astonished.

"But you do."

They wrote their initials on it with the date. Abram lit it and they waited for the right moment and released it by making a wish. They hugged each other and watched it fly until it disappeared. He gives her a forehead kiss. Their moment was interrupted by a phone call. Abram steps aside to answer it.

"Yes, thank you" saying so, he walks back to her. "Turn

around," he says.

"What?"

"I said turn around" he holds her hand trying to twirl her.

"Just stay" he blindfolds her.

"What are you doing, Abram?" She was curious.

"The night has just begun" he whispers, "Shall we go?"

She nods. They get back in the car and he drives them to the top of the hill. While Arshi remained in the car Abram steps out carrying food from the backseat. He places the food and lights candles around the place. He guides Arshi to the place and removes the blindfold. She stands in front of an astounding view with curtains wrapped around, launcher at the centre and surrounded by candles everywhere with a touch of lavender aroma. The candles placed in jars were hung to the branches of the tree making the place beautiful beyond words. Arshi was stunned and fell short of words.

"When did you do this? How did you do this? Wow!"

"I got this done.. for us." He smiled.

"Wow! You're good at this." She said, widening her adorable eyes.

"So, let's eat" he chuckled.

"What do you wanna have? Indian? Chinese? Italian? There's dessert for later." He said while looking in the boxes. When he gets no reply, he looks up to find her in teary eyes taking extra time noticing the details and him.

"What happened?" he sounded worried, "Are you okay?"

"Burgers. Burgers are good." She sniffed.

"The one with more cheese or less" and they argue for the one with more cheese.

Later they have Chinese too and share the dessert.

She laid down on Abram's arm under the starry sky. She clung to him. He caressed her fingers with his thumb as she spoke.

"These stars connect to form the shape of mango" she pointed to the sky and laughed. While she showed that, she saw something glow.

"Look Abram, a firefly." She ran after the firefly which leads the way to a dozen of them flying around.

"Why are you after it?" he questions.

"I haven't seen one in a long time."

"Do you want one?" He asked. She shook and looked at him with her winsome smile.

After many failed attempts he traps one in his fist and gets it to her. He hands it to her and she slowly takes a look and instantly clutches her fist when it tries to escape. Abram holds her hand and together they let it fly. They watch it find its group and glow with them.

"You're cold," he said, holding her in his arms. He takes out his blazer and covers her.

A cool breeze touches them calmly and it slowly starts to drizzle, putting off all the candles.

"Ah! Rain, just like our first date!" Arshi sighs.

"We can make this better." He winks.

"How?"

He walks swiftly to the car and plays a slow song. He walks to the tree beside the car and turns on the fairy lights. He had a backup in case it rains.

"Let's dance," he said, lending his hand. She nodded.

They danced to a slow song and later clung to each other and swung in sync to the music. They danced their heart out with the view of fairy lights, the rain and fireflies glowing around them.

She looked in his eyes and said, "I don't want this night to end."

"There will be many more nights like this." He assures me.

He opened the door for her and before she got in, she took one last look of the place to picture it forever. Sunset for her, stars for him and fireflies and fairy lights for both.

He drove them to their favourite place for ice cream. He ordered their regular, 2 chocolate ice creams for her and one for him. By the time she finished her ice creams, they reached her place.

He dropped her home and started to drive. He watched her through the rearview mirror as he turned. He stops the car, pulls the hand brake and runs into her arms and gives her a long hug like there's no tomorrow.

Promising to call her the minute she reaches home, he leaves.

November 8th, 2019

4:00 pm – Arshi wakes up from her sleep. It was the college bell, the end of last hour. She dumps all the books and pens she finds on the table, including her friends and hers. She and her friends share a look as she rushes to the corridor and her friends know exactly where she's going. She makes her way through the crowd and reaches the parking lot in a minute. She picks out the most beautiful flower among all the yellow flowers that bloom around the parking lot. She takes a glance to find Abram's bike.

She kisses the flower and places it under his helmet and walks far from the bike from where it is still visible. She waits patiently for him to come and notice it. She saw Abram last year at the college, a charming guy in a black T-shirt and blue jeans and she instantly fell in love with him. From the very next day, Arshi was regular and punctual to the college. Her eyes always searched for him. She would stand in the parking lot every day to get his one glimpse. Abram was very irregular and the day she would see him, the whole college would know that he was there.

She notices Abram from a long distance, her heart starts racing and the butterflies in her stomach flap their wings rapidly. He walks to his bike; he checks his phone and plugs in his AirPods. He lifts his helmet and notices a flower. Arshi hopes that he takes the flower with him instead he looks around and pushes the flower-like dust and wears his helmet. He starts his bike and drives away. When he flicked the flower, she felt her heart been thrown away. She stood there with tears in her eyes and a broken heart in her hand.

This is how Arshi celebrated her first anniversary with her crush, far different from the dream she had.

Aren't dreams a doorway to another realm, a glimpse into another life? Proof that we exist somewhere else... A parallel universe?

Aren't dreams trying to connect with you? Trying to tell you that your story is different in the parallel universe?

Arshi trusts that in the parallel universe they celebrated their first anniversary together. She believes that she looks into his eyes and holds his hand more often than looking at his picture in his world. She believes that they talk every night before they sleep unlike watching his picture every night hoping that they could at least be in the same room.

"The Arshi in the parallel universe might have spoken her heart out to Abram, maybe that's the reason I've nothing to tell him," she thought.

With these thoughts, Arshi turns around, plugs in her AirPods and plays 'Tu Jaane Na' from her playlist and walks away.

9

17.0 ERROR

BY SIDDHANTH RAJU

I t was day 17 of the adventure when Mack and Rorty had to make an unexpected stop.

Rorty- What happened Mack?

Mack- I guess we are out of space fuel...

Rorty- What do we do now?

Mack- I think I can use my 'portal gun' to find some alternative way out of here.

Rorty- I have been meaning to ask you something. How does this 'portal gun' of yours work?

Mack- It works on the principles of singularity of time, and its branches of parallel universes. And before you ask, I don't have time to explain what that is, we need fuel Rorty, fuel!

Rorty- [makes a sad face]

Mack- Don't make that creepy face... Wait. That face does remind me of a small-time writer I hired who was trying to get me to read his take on the concepts of parallel universe and stuff, Maybe that should work.

Rorty - Why did a scientist like you hire a writer?

Mack - Maybe you should stop with the questions and listen

to him, Rorty.

The following lines are a vague attempt to explain the readers and Rorty about the existence of a parallel universe and some other important fundamentals related to it.

"Relative, the word is relative," said The Writer to Rorty.

Then, he went on a long monologue, which looked like this.

"This word 'relative', why does it have so many meanings? For starters Einstein, the man, said that time is relative. Meaning, time flows differently for each person, excuse me, for each living thing. Sorry! For every object. My God! One last time let's do this correctly. Time flows differently for everything that has or will ever exist in this and all other known and unknown universes. Well, you are not reading this to understand Einstein equations, are you? You are here for an escapade, a journey in time and cosmos where these words will be your vehicle of imagination, sounds like Neil deGrasse Tyson didn't it? Well trying not to waste your time, let us take a small trip through the reality of time and a possibility that I may trick you into thinking that your life was never real, and neither is mine.

Do you believe in life? Of course, what is there to not believe in it, but do you believe in death? You know that death is inevitable, but you don't want to believe that do you? You for sure know that death can come in a second of your life in any form. You may start reading this and you may not read the next... line? Lucky huh! Or I may die while writing this story and never have a chance to submit it, well you know that didn't happen. I know some of you might cringe a little and say oh my god enough with the dead, aren't we hearing enough?"

"Well, to just put some light on the death (pun intended), every second on an average 1.8 humans die and 4.2 humans are born according to Guy Petzall in his research. He also concluded that there is a 0.464% chance that anyone including you and me can die this very second or this second depending on how many seconds it took for you to complete that sentence. So the minute you were born you had a 0.464% chance of dying so congratulations for making it this far. You might think that your odds turned out good, but have you ever thought that your grandparents had a lesser probability and they survived, let us go further back about 10 generations now looking at the proximity conditions, lack of technology, Education and Medical care their probability of survival was way less. So you mean to say that my lineage of 10 or 100 generations had a stroke of perfect luck in survival that I was born? Well, I wouldn't use the word luck. But how did it all turn out so well that you are here as a result of it, as a matter of fact, how do we know that it all did turn out well, we know that all of this was perfectly planned and are not just succeeding events that turn out as a repercussion for one mistake committed in the past, or is it. Did it all happen correctly? What is correct?

Correct is a state of mind, what was correct then might not be now and what is now might not be then and what is correct to you might not be to them and what is to me might not be to you, so are we all just a False to someone somehow somewhere sometime.

Or the Truth I am not here to argue about anybody's existence or give you an existential crisis we all suffer one unavoidably but as matter of fact you do know that your physical existence is based on your lineage of parents and grandparents and we know that it couldn't have been a perfect plan, according to the Bhagwat Geetha there has never been a deed that wasn't considered a mistake by someone but that doesn't mean you can't make them, Gods Devils Humans

Demons everyone makes mistakes that is the Kalachakra of life (wheel of time). And you me and this entire universe is a result of that mistake."

"Talking about mistakes, let us consider a moment in time, not a second, not a minute, not an hour, not a day, a moment, moment where a particular mistake is going to effect the next task that is going to happen a moment where it decides the fate of things that are going to happen for another 10 generations to come, I know what you are thinking, it's not that, you might think that this moment would be a huge life altering one , what an important moment it must have been, no it's not, it's not even that big, it's not even that important, it's just a thought, a thought that hit you when you were doing anything. Maybe your grandfather 11 by 11 here I mean 11 generations behind thought of getting married to someone else but at the final moment decided to marry your grandmother 11.

Well, that too is a very big example we have considered, according to fictional rules of time, even a small change in the mainstream of time can give birth to a lot of branches of timelines that would bend the principle time in annoying ways. This is where the concept of a parallel universe comes. It's not anything different from the usual reality, just wave your hand right now to any wall that is in front of you might seem a little weird to do but the fact is that you created a parallel universe. Every time a random possibility occurs a new parallel universe is created seems a bit tricky right. So, every time anything random happens that does not make sense a new universe is created? No, time acts a bit differently than that, time is like a little sapling and we are living in the parent branch. But as we know that a sapling in the process of becoming a tree it loses a lot of leaves and branches by natural causes so time grows and falls it's a natural process but that does not mean that the branches of time just grow and die all the time without a reason, the branches grow and die to teach the main branch to be perfect, as irritating it may sound yes time can't be perfect either it takes an enormous number of parallaxes to fix it and to be perfect, Parallaxes can sound like bad leaves or branches but they are important, the sapling of time is constantly changing , but the change is what makes the flow of time near to perfect."

"So that's it, that is the explanation on time and its cause of parallel universes, so let's get a fast recap ,time runs differently for everything, parallel universes are created whenever there is a difference in singularity, and they are destroyed to keep the sapling of time alive. Now we are all caught up, talking about Singularity we should see how this singularity of time is affecting us since it is something that affects everyone. According to the work of Robert Jastrow, the whole universe is nothing but a very big painting and all that is happening now is happening on a two-dimensional canvas, it was a very peculiar theory I suppose, but why did he stop there if the universe is painting then every other multiverse or parallel universe is a brush stroke being added to this painting just to make this a perfect masterpiece? To think of it are there other paintings, are there other artists painting their own pictures or is this the only one happening, all these questions arrive only when we try to derive/or understand the concept of what Jastrow said when we try to disintegrate and break it into simple equations, speaking of equations.

Derive, Rorty, equations are to be derived. Peculiar word isn't it, the word means to find logical proof of a theoretical sentence or statement. Yet it doesn't ever end. There is no finite derivation to anything if you look at the value of PI 3.1415926535.... but to make our calculations easy we take

3.14 so we have a definite value of PI, so to measure something we have to stop at a particular point but isn't that just an approximate value, so basically everything that can be measured is just an approximate value then does That mean even time is just an approximate value, you are measuring it aren't you, you may think that what does the value of pie have to do with time, Well look at an analogue clock right now what is it shaped like a circle right! The path that is traced by the hour and minute hands are a circle why stop there the earth on who's rotation time is measured isn't the path traced by it a sphere so what we are concluding I'm sorry, what do we observe, that the physical measurement of time is just an approximate value and there is no other way I mean If I could take all matter on this earth convert it into ink put it in a pen and use this whole universe as my paper to keep deriving the value of PI it would not stop, Is this why time also doesn't stop, Maybe but have you ever stopped and asked this question that why are we measuring time why are we dividing 22 by 7?"

"I mean things remain constant rather finite until we start to derive things, does that mean that the universe is constant until we try to derive it, of course it is what a childish question, would that mean anything is a constant until it is derived and it leaves the state of eternal constancy only when it is added, subtracted, multiplied, divided, differentiated or integrated with another value so does that mean that time to needs another entity another value and it can't exist on its own? If time is 22 then what is the 7, is it the multiverses? I mean, there are sayings/Vedas/verses in many Spiritual books that there are 7 other worlds that exist above and below the main singularity of real time, is there a link, well spirituality has its own different take on the theory of multiverse and parallel universes, but the basic ideology has always come from noticing something that has already happened. Chrysippus the first man to ever talk or start the idea of a parallel universe used the process of determinism to support his arguments, the concept of determinism simply states that the existence of anything depends upon the things that have existed before it, in simple terms something that is existing now is due to something that was existing before so there is a slight chance that the spiritual concept does have an important role in determining the scientific solution of time. They do say that science and religion are two faces of a coin and you can't see them both together; but have you ever thought that you need both these sides to form the coin both have to exist together to be one?"

"I personally feel that humans use science as a tool to discover religion and he is proud to believe that religion helped him. This debate on Spirituality and science is for another day but for now let us get back to our point of interest the multiverse, so we have read that there is nothing new if the knowledge of multiverse exists ,it was discovered before so if we have time I mean if we get back to the beginning of time according to Chrysippus and his ideology of Determinism something has to exist before for something to exist now so if time started at the point and it has been running till now does that mean something existed before time actually started for it to exist now, so what existed before time was it more time what existed before the universe was it another universe I mean it is said and believed that everything is born from something then what is time born from, So are we just a painting or are we just a marble in that supreme forces hand. And is time just an approximation of the life that we are leading, are we even the parent branch of the sapling or just a branch that is waiting for the right moment to fall off."

R- I see you are back with the Space fuel.

M- Yes, so Rorty, did this wannabe writer so called trick you into believing that you don't exist? He can be very dramatic with his words.

R- True that, but I don't know Mack, I still think, and I do believe that I exist. I don't know if the world we are living in is the real timeline, but you can't change the fact that you are living in it. It may be until the branch falls but we sure can live it to our fullest and enjoy every second of what we have.

M - So, you haven't understood a word. Sigh! Rorty, let's just continue with our adventure. I don't want to waste this writer's work.

R- How is it wasted? I did learn and understand a lot of things, and I really liked his work.

M- I hope they liked it too.

10

GIRL AND HER CLOSET OF DREAMS

BY AMY GRACE

J ust like any other day, on a quiet morning, the birds continued chirping, which was the first thing that woke her up at 3:30 AM from sleep. Those tiny sparrows near her window did not stop chirping from 3 AM in the dawn, their efforts were finally successful as she is awake now wondering how quiet it is outside despite those continuous chirping.

She started enjoying their songs, dancing to their tune and she wasn't cranky because her sleep is disturbed but she was glad and felt loved. She said to herself that it's about time to reflect on something in her life.

She is Kira, her life is quite normal just like that morning but something inside her is waking her up, a whisper, a knowing from inside that she needs to move to the city next to her town, but she's not ready yet. Those little birdies next to her window helped her to understand that she needs to take the next step in her life and she's going to enjoy the ride, after all the best decisions of our lives often need constant reminders.

Now Kira is a girl who's very good at her studies and she's full of endless dreams and passion. She's a helper, a great friend to everyone who crosses her path, a listener, a big time-avid reader, loves to bake, loves kids. But like many of us, she has quite some insecurities and mistakes which are holding her back from her life ahead, life in a prestigious medical college in the city. After all the counselling from everybody around her right from her friends to family to her neighbours, she wasn't convinced. Then these little birdies helped her to decide that she's moving out as she was led to open a scripture that reads "You are the light of the world. A city set on a hill cannot be hidden."- Matthew 5:14 ESV

It stuck with her because one of the meanings for her name Kira is Shine. Other meanings are a beam of light and ruler of people. Not only is she the light of the world, but God reminded her that she is like a city set on a hill which cannot be hidden. Meaning God is her source of survival, wherever she is. That helped her to take a step further.

The day when she had to leave the house had finally come, she packed all her belongings, everything that she even packed her dreams in a closet of her soul. As much as she wanted to be a doctor, she dreamt of being a theatre artist who can act on stages - live-action, a journalist, a crafter and a host for a cooking show, the list of her crazy things go on which she'll never share with anyone. Because she's afraid of the label that she's too greedy. Greedy of dreaming/ wanting to play too many roles. As most of her friends say to her that she should be just happy with the doctor seat as a few qualify to get it. But her heart wants to be more than just a doctor who heals the bodies, she wants to be someone who heals the souls and touches their spirit with every ounce of her to point them to the Creator and Savior.

Nonetheless, she keeps shut with the people but goes crazy with her father in prayer sharing every bit of her heart because she knows she's in safe hands.

She had joined the college, made good friends, acing her exams and learning well. But her dreams were all locked up in a closet waiting to be opened only by her. She was up late-night till 3 AM. The one who used to wake up from sleep around that time is now going to sleep at the very same time. A lot of her habits have been changed, but suddenly to her notice, she saw a small birdie next to her study room, chirping exactly in the same notes on the day she made her biggest decision of her life. But this time it flew away quickly, it did not leave her in peace.

Lying on a bed, closing her eyes, not sleeping, squeezing the pillow next to her, she went to the closet of her dreams, with her keys of possibility. She thought to herself if, at all a parallel universe where she could be everything she wanted to ever exist, she didn't want to miss that chance. She took a deep breath as she opened the closet and dived into the day where she would be all of the things that she ever wanted to be.

For the starters: She was one of the famous theatre artists - fulltime, everybody applauded her for her work as she poured her life to the characters she played and she felt content in her shoes, she worked hard for it enjoying all the highs and lows it has to offer.

Then she turned into a full-time journalist, who's very loyal at her job, providing the right news and relevant news following the anthem of Satya Meva Jayatey (truth alone wins), no matter what.

A perfect handmade crafter who would turn people's dreams into reality using her painting, sculpting skills serving people's love.

As I said the list goes on, she tried every role she ever wanted to be. And she imagined, to be all things at once.

Then she heard the birdie chirping again, she opened her

eyes to look around. Nothing is changed, she's the same old Kira but something inside her stirred up.

This time she reflected on all the possibilities, she understood that if she could be everything, she wanted to be all at once, would be so traumatic for a person to endure.

She reasoned her life that the purpose of a person is more important than the roles we choose to play. Purpose of our life should not change ever. Now she's a doctor, in reality, to serve others. In her hoped reality, she played as an artist, journalist, crafter but still her purpose remained the same, to serve people with entertainment, right information and love. She discovered that the consequences of her hoped reality might be tiring on her and the potential she has to offer this world and learnt that.

She can be everything she wanted to be by learning at her own pace but not all at once.

She needs to take everything bit by bit, changing her hoped reality into the possibility in God-ordained way.

She trusted God even more now that his purpose will prevail in her life more than her plans and hoped reality.

She realized that she's not greedy for wanting to be more than just one thing.

She learnt if everything goes as per one wish, we fail to appreciate the efforts involved.

But this time, she did not block her closet of dreams but surrendered them to God's hands, hoping that he would bring one by one into her life. Just like her how she moved to the city for the first time.

For a change she started to conquer her dreams one by one, she hand sculpted a sparrow to remind her that despite the situations outside, quiet or quarrelsome. The whispers of her

Lord, being led by his Spirit is all she needs to have in her life.

She joined a theatre art course to pursue her acting skills part-time.

She started reading and researching more about real stuff that people need to hear.

Started sharing them as news updates.

She started baking and teaching younger kids.

She told herself lyrics of one of her favourite songs - goes by, baby steps my friend, to you it may be nothing, but it makes daddy proud.

She started investing her time into all the activities, soon she realized that she's missing out on her academics.

That made her give up on all her dreams, nothing mattered to her anymore.

The time's ticking away. She thought to herself that the reality she hoped is slipping away from her hands. The more she tried, the more tired she became.

She didn't want to risk her reality for the sake of hoped reality. Yet she truly believed for it to happen someday.

Lost in her thoughts sitting on a terrace, with her books open gazing on dark clouds, which are about to break and rain. She heard a little birdie chirping again, she remembered all the times when her God was faithful and didn't fail her. That gave her immense hope that she cried her heart out as it was raining, she brought down the books and enjoyed the view from the corridor. She heard the chirping of a birdie getting amplified as the rain poured out with heavy thunders. Suddenly it stopped as the little birdie found her nest to rest.

That made her realize that she needs to find rest and peace even in the turmoil of her life to continue to have her own hoped reality.

She found her peace in her Lord. Everything is back to normal again, she started preparing well for her exams and aced them.

She learnt that for her hoped reality is beyond her reach in her abilities, but it can be possessed when lived at the right time, right happenings in right believing.

Everything needs its own time, and we need to prioritize the time to achieve anything in our life.

As she was on her journey, she realized the power of teamwork. She started sharing her ideas and thoughts to the like-minded people to encourage and mentor her in the right direction she needs to take. She learnt that the right company, right people, right leaders and right mentors will always help you grow better and lift you in the hardest times of your life. They voluntarily invest their time into your life because they believe in you more than yourself, they want you to see yourself the right way, how God made you.

She started gaining skills one after the other, she started serving people through her profession.

One fine day when the chirping birdie came and sat peacefully on her shoulder. She said to herself,

"Everybody wants to live a life where anything is possible, but when we don't see that happening, we close our eyes, mostly the closets of our hearts which carry a gazillion desires and dreams.

Not knowing that it's okay to not have our hoped reality at the very moment. But if we continue in persistence and never give up, we might be fortunate enough to see it manifest one day. But all that matters is to have peace at every turn of our life be it in reality or hoped reality."

Those little birdies always reminded her along the way the scripture that read.

"Look at the birds of the air: they neither sow nor reap nor gather into barns, and yet your heavenly Father feeds them. Are you not of more value than they?"- Matthew 6:26 ESV

Her value and worth are found not in the roles she plays or who she is, but it lies in the fact of Whose she is. She's God's darling daughter in Christ.

She will continue to keep her closet of dreams open to reach out to the other world of possibilities, but she won't fail to live one here as her father in heaven always backs her up.

In her hoped reality, she wanted to be everything she dreamt of, she's passionate and working hard for them she was succeeding without pressure. But in reality, she is best or trying to be best at one thing that is nurturing the things she has in her hands at the present moment but still is under constant pressure.

Taking things one by one and focusing on one thing at a time without being under pressure is the secret she has mastered over time by grace and wisdom of God. She found her peace and the rest in him.

For a girl in the city, reality or hoped reality had many differences but one thing remained the same. That is her God.

She trusted her God in this one thing:

"Now to him who can do far more abundantly than all that we ask or think, according to the power at work within us." - Ephesians 3:20 ESV

11

MECHANICAL DREAMS

BY C.L. WILLIAMS

Devon is awakened and is sent to an empty room where he awaits the person he only knows as "Doctor". The doctor needs to check Devon for progress and updates as the Doctor has noticed changes, good and bad, in Devon. The truth is, Devon is trying to progress in the way Doctor needs him to, but Devon has also fallen in love and even though he has difficulties processing or showing other emotions, he knows he is in love.

Devon is void of any other feeling. It is why Doctor knows there is no need to apologize to Devon once the checkup takes place as Doctor knows Devon will show no emotion about having to wait.

"Hello Devon," the Doctor says, walking into the room.

"Hello Doctor," Devon responds.

"I would apologize for my delay, but I already know your understanding of my apology does not comply with you." The doctor tells Devon.

"I understand you are late; I also understand that I am not the only one you need to check upon. Therefore, there is no need to apologize to me." Devon explains.

The doctor grabs a clipboard and begins writing down a summary of the current conversation with Devon. This is the first time Doctor knows that Devon has shown understanding. Doctor jots a few more notes before putting the clipboard down to ignite a conversation with Devon.

"Devon," the Doctor begins. "I've noticed you have equal progression with your brother Aevon. I've noticed you two progress in different categories. What are your thoughts on this?"

"Well, Aevon and I are brothers. Therefore, we excel in different things to complement one another. I know his speech is better than mine, yet I have better motor skills than he does. May I show you?" Devon extends his hand.

The doctor removes the note page from the clipboard and hands the clipboard and a pen to Devon. Devon takes the pen and begins drawing a picture. Once finished, Devon hands the clipboard and pen back to Doctor.

"I see you've drawn a picture of Kaley." The doctor observes, "May I ask why you chose to draw a picture of her over anyone else? I noticed you began drawing this the second I handed you the pen. You already knew you were going to draw her."

"She is always nice to me and mentions I have a big heart. I apologize that my drawing isn't the best. It's hard to draw a glowing smile when my only tool is a black ink pen." Devon responds.

"Devon, I asked why you chose to draw Kaley over anyone else here. Why did you choose to draw her?" Doctor asks once again.

"Doctor, I did tell you why. I told you that she is always nice to me and talks about my big heart." Devon explains.

"I'm nice to you." The doctor points out.

"You are nice; however, I do believe you are upset with my current progressions. You also never mention my big heart. Kaley is the only one here that ever mentions my big heart."

The doctor grabs the notes from earlier and jots down a few more things. The truth is, Doctor does believe Devon and Aevon should have further progressions than they currently do. However, Devon and Aevon have progressed in areas that others have yet to and it is why Doctor does not show any disappointments. The doctor is curious as to why Devon enjoys Kaley's presence more than the others that visit him. The doctor places the clipboard down and exits the room. Devon goes from observant to a resting position.

Devon remains in the resting position until Doctor returns. The doctor opens the door and greets Devon.

"Devon, I'm back." The Doctor tells him.

"I'm aware. Welcome back, Doctor." Devon responds.

"I also brought a friend with me." The doctor tells Devon. "Come on in."

After the Doctor says come on in, Devon is greeted by Kaley, his crush. Devon tries his best to greet Kaley but gets tongue-tied as he starts speaking.

"Kaley, how are you? I mean, hi!" An embarrassed Devon finally speaks.

"Hi Devon," Kaley says to Devon as she puts her hand on Devon's chest. "There's that big heart of yours." Kaley looks at Devon and smiles.

"Thank you!" Devon responds.

"Devon drew this picture of you earlier today when I asked him to show me his improved motor skills." The doctor grabs the drawing from his clipboard and hands it to Kaley.

"Devon! I love it!" Kaley smiles and kisses Devon on the cheek. "I have work to do but I'll be back. Bye Doctor. Bye Devon." Kaley exits.

The doctor sees the look upon Devon's face and asks him, "Devon, are you going into dream mode?" Before the Doctor can realize the words he just said, Devon activates Dream Mode.

"Dream mode activated!" Devon slips into Dream Mode.

Devon gets up and leaves the Doctor alone in the room. He marches his way to Kaley's office and opens the door without knocking. At first, Kaley is upset but once she sees it's Devon that's entering without an invitation, she settles down.

"Hello, Devon. How are you?" Kaley asks.

"I am good now that I am alone in this room with you." Devon is straightforward with his intentions, making Kaley blush in the process.

"Devon, those are some strong words. Are you trying to tell me something?" A red-faced Kaley asks.

"Yes, I am saying I want to spend more time with you, alone, and not in this place!" Devon says as he extends his hand to Kaley.

Kaley does not hesitate; she grabs Devon's hand and the two of them leave and within seconds are in the open field at the local park. The first place Kaley took Devon when trying to check his motor skills. "This is where we first met. It has..." Devon pauses as he isn't sure of the correct word to say, "Value, to me. I hope this place will have value for us." He says as he turns and looks at Kaley in her bright blue eyes.

"I think you are trying to say something special to me, Devon," Kaley mentions.

"You told me I have a big heart. No one has mentioned my heart before. That is until you came along." Devon says as his pitch gets higher and his heart rate begins to increase. Devon tries to think of the right words to say to her, but his mind keeps running blank. Devon stops thinking and grabs his crush by the waist and pulls her closer towards him. Devon decides to go for it and kisses her.

Their lips separate and Devon is now looking at a blushing Kaley, she is also at a loss for words. She just smiles at him with her cheeks painted pink. She wants to tell him her feelings are mutual but decides to kiss him once more. After a second passionate kiss, Kaley breaks the silence. "I've always had feelings for you Devon," she says as she leans in and kisses him on the cheek. "I wish I could have told you about my feelings sooner. I thought telling you about how much I like your big heart was enough. I should've been more direct with you."

"We have right now. We have this moment. For me, for us, that is what matters." Devon responds.

"What do you want to do now, Devon?" Kaley asks.

"I only want to spend time with you as I hold you in my arms," Devon responds.

"Let's just go back to my place and watch some television while I'm loved by the warmth that is you."

Devon leans in and kisses Kaley one more time. This time, the sensation of their lips touching is euphoric. The feeling of time stopping as Devon is intertwined with his one true love. They spend the day together until she takes him home with her.

The two of them are now together, alone in Kaley's house. The two of them share some small talk before Kaley puts on a movie. The two of them are only pretending to watch the movie because deep down the two of them want intimacy with one another. After a few minutes of "watching the movie", Devon moves closer to Kaley and puts his arm around her. She quickly moves in closer and holds Devon's hand that's closest to her. After a few minutes of cuddling, Kaley moves up and gives Devon a quick kiss. The two look at one another with love in their eyes. Devon brushes Kaley's hair from her face, puts his hand on her face, noticing the smooth feeling of her skin. He smiles at her, she smiles back, and that's when he moves in to kiss her. His kiss is far more passionate as it is more than just a simple peck. He places his arms around her as the two are now lying on Devon's couch, not far from making love.

"Devon," Kaley whispers into his ear, "I am all yours."

Devon starts to lean in and kiss Kaley once more, but a voice stops him.

"Devon!" The voice projects.

"What's wrong Devon?" Kaley asks.

"I'm hearing voices," Devon explains.

"Devon!" The voice lets out a louder projection.

Devon does his best to ignore the voice, but it's too strong.

"DEVON!" The voice screams out one more time. This time, Devon is no longer at Kaley's house, cuddling with his crush. He is back in the room with the Doctor, who is ready to run diagnostics.

"Devon, are you back?" Doctor asks.

"Yes," Devon responds. "I am no longer in dream mode."

"Ok, I need to run some diagnostics on you and make sure you don't fall into dream mode when either of those words is said. Got it?" Doctor explains.

"Understood." Devon sits there while waiting for the

diagnostics to run. After a few minutes, Devon says, "Diagnostics complete."

After the diagnostics are finished, Devon looks through the window of the room he is in and sees Kaley with a group of kids leading them on a tour. She is showing the kids Devon's brother Aevon. Devon's lip-reading is minimal, but he can tell she respects his brother. She notices a kid raising their hand and Kaley is quick to answer the question for the child. She smiles and leads the kids into the next room, the room he is in.

"This, kids, is Aevon's twin brother, Devon," Kaley says as she starts talking about Devon.

"How can robots have siblings?" A child asks without raising their hand.

"Devon and Aevon were made from the same metals and fiber optics. These two were the only ones to share material as the other robots were made from different materials from one another. Since Devon and Aevon were made from the same metals, they are brothers." Kaley turns her attention towards Devon, "Isn't that right Devon?"

"Correct!" Devon responds.

Kaley walks over to Devon and opens up his battery chamber, revealing the insides of the machine being on the table. "This is Devon's operating system. As you can see, compared to the other robots you have seen today, Devon's operating system is much larger. You can say Devon has the biggest heart of any robot in this building." Kaley looks at Devon and smiles before leading the kids to the dining area for lunch.

Devon watches as his crush continues her job of showing others around the robotics building. He knows she's good at her job, but he still wishes for a moment alone with her to tell her how he feels. He wants to do more than just a basic drawing on a piece of paper. He wants her to know that even though he isn't human, he can love her better than anyone else. He wants to make her fall in love with him. Deep down, Devon just wants his mechanical dreams to one day, become a reality.

12

CONCEALED FANTASY UNFORESEEN REALITY

BY HARSHA SHINDE

Like a newborn who opens her eyes into the world new to her, I opened mine. Unable to adjust with the surroundings, my eyelids fluttered rapidly.

I felt my body getting crushed under the abstract pain that shot all over me. I wasn't able to move my hands or legs, nor could I move my fingers. Luckily, the blindness vanished, and I saw Saurav, my elder brother, sitting next to me. I had never seen him like this - his eyes were swollen, hair all messed up and seemed drained out.

I tried to lift my head and saw him massaging my feet but couldn't feel a thing.

"Meher, can you hear me?" I could feel the pain in his voice.

I tried to respond, but my mind and body didn't coordinate. Whatever happened at the townhouse must have mutilated my nervous system. I've been facing several hallucinations since.

I just saw Saurav in my ward, now just his face, now only his teary eyes and, everything just blacked out.

***

No! I cried out in agony as my brain burned, my joints cracked, fingers trembled yet I stood up despite the pain and anguish. Where am I?

I took steps towards the only thing that caught my attention in a dark room, a silver shining door. Amidst the darkness, I tried to take every step with caution. I opened the door, it made a screeching sound as if it hadn't been closed for months; whoa! How did I come here then?

I held the door open before closing it to see what it looks like in the light. There were candles scattered and their molten wax all over the floor. Books were all messed up; none was on the shelf where it was meant to be, maybe it's a library at home.

I closed it, climbed the compact staircase which after a floor led me to a huge drawing-room. I'm trying to find my way out of here yet with every step I enter a new place.

I looked across the drawing-room searching for the main entrance, for my exit.

Mom? I saw her sitting on a couch, her back facing me as I wandered across the hall.

"Mom, what are you doing?" I don't know what should astonish me more, the fact that why is she here or what is doing with a Grimoire.

"Meher, are you feeling alright now? You got out of the library I see" she exclaimed as she hugged me.

"Ahem I guess" I simply pulled away.

"Now go to your room and freshen up we have to complete the ritual" consoling me she continued to read the grimoire.

Go to your room? This is my house??!!?

Except for the staircase that led me to this huge, rustic drawing-room; I could just see one at the left corner in front of the main entrance door. I climbed the stairs up to the second floor, I turned right, there was a huge lobby and to my left at a certain distance were multiple doors to different rooms. There were at least 4 until I found the one named after me 'Meher'.

I entered it; everything was properly arranged. The pretty millennial pink wallpaper in combination with the off-white-coloured wall brightened that room, no, my room; I corrected myself.

I don't know why my mind is so messed up right now everything seems peculiar. My room didn't feel like it's mine. I roamed around to have a proper look at it.

I opened my wardrobe, pulled out a white full sleeve's turtleneck top with a mini black denim skirt, placed it on my bed and went to have a nice warm shower.

I got ready and headed downstairs. I kind of liked the way I was feeling, everything seemed familiar, but I couldn't completely accept it.

"Granny" I gushed, halting my thoughts and rushed towards the rocking chair she was seated in and hugged her tightly. The fact that my family didn't seem distant to me like my house, comforted me.

"Look at you, my sweet girl all dressed up for her big day" she exclaimed.

"Once we complete the ritual you will officially be a witch with complete power to fight evil. Amaira unknowingly blessed you with exceptional power, I envy that though," mom interrupted, and her every word took me by surprise.

"What ritual? Who Amaira? And witches?!??!" my confusion was visible.

"You don't remember anything, do you? First, honey, you

are a witch, that's the world we live in. This world carries magic which is channelled in some chosen families. Luckily, ours is one of them. We have a hold of this entire town, and so we have many foes too. That's the reason we kept you spellbound in the basement, in the library which can't be broken until you are ready to perform magic and stays till your transition is completed. You did come out of there, so now you are ready", this explanation made zero sense, but the ongoing events made me believe it, like how I came here if I was on the hospital bed earlier.

To settle my curiosity I asked, "Who's a threat to me that you felt the need to conceal me in the basement?"

Granny took over "Amaira, your mom's cousin, she used black magic to bring her daughter back to life for which she is cursed for an eternity of misery and needs the sacrifice of a new witch to undo it. Also, when I said she unknowingly blessed you with power, I meant she came for you. We couldn't fight her, and she did a locator spell with 100 more witches and partially broke the spell I put around you. You couldn't face that much power and absorbed the excess, moreover, lay there half unconscious and half damaged" this is insane, everything she just said.

"What do you mean by damaged?"

"You weren't completely dead, Saurav sacrificed himself in the ritual to save you" each word brought equal astonishment.

"To save you we needed young magic and blood, Saurav sacrificed to save you. He's no more" those last three words hurt my ears.

***

No can't be, I saw Saurav. He's not dead. My head was burning, what was happening to me. Saurav! I screamed.

"Meher, what happened?", I heard his voice. I opened my eyes; I was in the hospital, Saurav right by my side. The previous pain seemed to vanquish at the sight of him. I lifted myself, hugged him tightly.

"Whoa jerry you're okay, I see the medicines finally worked", I could feel his happiness but not him.

"You know granny said you're dead", I cried in his shoulders.

"Granny said? She passed away in that accident. Also, Mom and Dad, our mansion is destroyed too. Are you having dreams again?" he pulled back wiping my tears.

What's happening? Did the world just turn upside down? That wasn't a dream I know for sure. Our house which Saurav said was destroyed, I walked there just now. The people he said are dead, I just met them. Granny said Saurav sacrificed himself to save me while I was lying in the library unconscious.

How is this even happening, one moment I'm at one place and the next I'm somewhere else.

Granny said I was not completely dead but somewhat dead, that means I was temporary on the other side where every supernatural being goes after death? Or am I on the other side right now? How can I live in two different places rather than dimensions at the same time?

Am I still partly dead and partly alive? If so, which one of the two is the actual world?

***

There are candles lit all around me, maybe just at a foot's distance. I felt the heat on my skin as I looked around; it's the library. I'm simultaneously reappearing at different places.

Granny, Mom, Dad and some faces I didn't recognize surrounded me in a circle chanting some spells, the candles ignited in a boom, I screamed and jumped up, just then the fire blew off.

"Are you trying to burn me alive? What is happening to me?" I yelled as loud as I could and crashed on the marble floor crying my eyes out. The last place I was in this house was the drawing-room where I heard the lie of Saurav of not being alive and now again in the library.

"Calm down, we are completing the ritual to complete your transition. You have the utmost power right now than any of us, don't move, stay still. Your actions can have severe consequences", some witch warned me when everyone re-kindled the candles and started their spells.

"How am I supposed to calm down? You have no idea what's happening to me. You say my brother is dead, he says you guys are dead", all my suppressed rage, confusion and helplessness were on board. I stood up, threw my hands in the air and yelled 'stop it', as loudly as I could. Everyone was thrown away, windows broke, the fire went off and the marbled floor cracked also not to mention the torturing spells stopped at once.

"Oh My God! What just happened?" I no more felt weak or helpless; I felt powerful like, just my actions could change anything. Right now, what I did, that was hard to digest it myself, well at least for the old me, jumping from one dimension to another with no idea how the hell that is possible.

My powers affected my brain; I strangely enjoyed those though and believed in magic.

Saurav? He's not here but I saw him wherever I was before. That felt real, hell I was there breathing the same air as he did to stay alive, I'm feeling the same here. All that matters is he is alive no matter which dimension. I can reunite my family with my powers or as Granny calls, magic. I just have to figure out which is the world of the living-living and which one of the living dead.

"Now that I have magic and the so-called transition you were completing is done. So with magic, I can bring Saurav back from where he is to reunite with us, or we can reunite with him. I mean magic can do any damn thing, right? Also, I'm stronger than any of you here" I let out my excitement with each word I uttered, and everyone was slowly getting up on their feet shooting me angry glances. They can't harm me, so I don't care how angry they are with me.

"No, the last part of your transition to a real witch is still on hold for which you need to kill one witch and absorb their power, but you shoved us off, you still don't have total control of your magic. Also, a point to be noted, magic isn't some child's play, there's a reason why you are given access to magic once you become mature enough around 17-18 years of age. It's all about natural balance, bringing a dead person implies to break the law, which has consequences as severe as an eternity of misery or torched death. Mother Earth helps, but also punishes the lawbreakers and believe me none other than your Mother knows this the best", an adamant witch probably a couple of years younger than mom fired a gist of the severity of my magic and how it works also she emphasized on last words.

"Bring back the dead? Well, I'm not sure where the dead are. Maybe you guys are dead or Saurav, respectively in your freaking different world or I am dead wandering to complete different dimensions; that is, there's no more life, everyone's dead, it is the end', I lost my temper.

IT IS THE END; I said it plainly but how can there be an end I'm living, several other people are or, are we the living dead? Just because I can't figure out who is dead and alive doesn't imply an end or probably for me it is; either way, if this is the land of the living my normal magic-free life has ended if it's not my life is truly over.

The balance! between living and dead that witch said; this, suddenly popped in my mind which means on either of the two sides people are alive. This is not the end then.

"Sweetie listens to me, not everyone is dead. You are hyper thinking just because you have excess power, nowhere to channel than your brain. You are alive; this ritual is partially to bring you to consciousness from the magic you absorbed when Amaira tried to take you down and, partly for bringing magic to you. Let's complete it at once and as soon as possible." Mom caressed my face, and I sensed a warning to do as she says.

"Okay", I agreed.

Their spells started, the candles fumed, and my head felt heavy. I also noticed my nose bleeding. Soon after that, I collapsed on the floor.

***

I opened my eyes still lying on the hospital bed, Saurav by my side.

My ward's door opened and we both yearned to know who might visit us at night.

"Mom, Dad .... Granny?" I was perplexed. Are they also travelers travelling two dimensions like me?

"I thought you didn't survive the gas leak, the reports said so," Saurav was surprised.

"Yes, we didn't but also you, Saurav. Sometimes foes pretend to be our friends until their face under the mask is revealed. I hope Meher is safe, luckily, she wasn't home. We may live multiple times but die once", mom replied.

Everything came to me as a terrible shock. What's happening?

"Mom, I just saw you guys at our house." I said immediately.

She didn't reply, "Mom! Dad! Hey, can't you hear me? Saurav?"

No one answered, can't they see me?

Who saved me? 'Sometimes foes appear to be friends' and, 'We may live multiple times but die once', mom's exact words.

Two lives don't imply two separate deaths when one ceases to exist in a dimension, the events round up to end your life in the other world.

Foe, I guess I know who...

****

I opened my eyes into the library I lay in, completing my transition. I blew off the candles from which those witches drew energy by raising my hands as if I'm pushing someone and my power hurled them down.

"Amaira, I know it's you disguised as my mom, I guess black magic is handy to you. Also, you don't care about this ritual, you just need my power to undo your curse", I continued the spells to unleash the real selves of all those witches around me. They couldn't fight me, except one, Amaira who at least tried to but, a mind driven from revenge is much stronger than that which craves power.

"You will die with me; I linked our lives beforehand; I die you die. Now, this is the end of your magic, this world and you. The world collapses with the death of the powerful, which is you", it was too late to stop; I couldn't control my powers, with her last words I took my last breath.

I was supposed to die today, and I did; the protection spell, granny said it will stay till my ritual is completed which was halted due to Amaira.

At the same time to complete it, I needed a witch's blood on my hand; I killed Amaira.

The so prolonged ritual is finally completed, my family saved me twice and the most awaited moment finally arrived. I'm a witch now.

Everything made sense as if I connected every loose end.

Surprisingly though, I found myself lying on the same hospital bed but none of my family members were around. Was it an illusion?

I felt the power, not just mentally but also intellectually realizing there is just one other side for the dead according to their doings of the respective reality they live in, one of their afterlives is in hell and other in heaven. No one is pure, everyone sins some point. During both the lives, one which is severely sinned goes to hell other to heaven. They never meet, I guess that's why we believe there's only one world as the other is concealed.

My family was dead all this time, they couldn't face Amaira's power yet helped me through, they guided me all along as my guardian angels.

From the beginning, I believed one is the land of the living and the other of the dead. Whereas I was alive in two different places at the same time but under different conditions. I was a witch and a human in respective worlds. Two similar bodies dodging themselves between parallel universes.

Partially alive as a witch and a human, that caused sheer chaos it disrupted the two parallel threads of two different universes. That's the reason I glitched. My body was just equalizing the balance of the universe.

The realization that followed was scary. I couldn't find myself in one piece as I realized what exactly had happened. Or maybe I glitched due to the supernatural abnormality and could feel my concurrent presence of both worlds unknowingly travelling one Place to Another.

One universe to another.

13

A NEW HOME

BY RAGA LAHARI

Today, the world will see a new window, Honey, I murmured to myself while my name was being announced very loud and clear. I took just four steps forward, climbed another four steps onto the stage and walked straight to the podium, my excitement and nervousness wrapped together while all the flashlights were pointed right at me. From the top, I could see many puzzled faces in the media. The curiosity in the room was very contagious, not to mention at an overwhelming pace. There was pin-drop silence, yet I could sense the mess in the audience's minds.

I heard the speaker's voice, "Mrs. Darim, please can you go ahead and share your recent experiences with us about it?" I sensed a different feeling, as though I was about to be acknowledged as someone odd. Immediately, I took three deep breaths, meanwhile holding the mike tightly. I said without fumbling, "Sure. Good Morning, I am Kara Darim, a psychologist at the country's capital sector psychology unit. My husband was Mr. Broon Darim, a scientist, Robotics unit." I felt like I heard a different voice, very different from my own, while I kept talking on the mic. My brain was producing numerous visuals which were crystal clear to me.

My soul felt I was about to relive a past that I didn't know how to explain. Yet I decided to go on with my story. "He had a passion for research on robots. He always asked me, 'If I were a robot, would you still live with me?' and we automatically laughed looking at each other's faces. One fine afternoon, I received a phone call from him, and a nurse said, "Mrs. Darim, Sorry. It's bad news. Number 17, Morgue ward, Tonic Hospitals. Hurry up!" I left my subject's test score sheets on the desk, handed over the lab keys at the office and rushed to my destination at once. After I saw him, my brain felt a shock wave being passed. He was lying on the bed, wearing a shocked expression on his face, not moving an inch. The nurse handed over a piece of paper to me, as though it was something precious.

"Brown letter in my cabin locker. I'm sorry but trust me, I love you," I read. My heart understood that those were his final words. I was given a warm pat on my shoulder and the speaker said, "Here, have some water." I took some sips and kept quiet. One of the journalists there asked me, "What was in the letter? Did you look for it after he passed away?" A cop from the audience asked, "How did your husband die?" The speaker asked, "Are you feeling alright, ma'am?" I did not listen to more questions and quickly jumped to explain what was in the letter. "I found some research result papers which had information on how to activate the robot that he had been creating over all these years. There was a document marked in red which said that this project must be stopped forever because of the intense danger it imposes on the scientist while building it.

Next, I found his signature on a document giving his statement that he is willing to continue his experiments on the robot even if it meant he would die. There were some more papers on instructions and safety precautions, the robot's working period and limitations, mathematical formulae and results, and some other details about more equipment. I was shattered, yet immensely proud of him and his work. I was restless for quite a long period but decided on our anniversary that I would not let his passion and work go in vain. Quickly, I read all the details and was prepared firmly to activate his lifetime dream. I thought I had to soon name the robot after activating it. The robot structure was one of his masterpieces. It looked just like any other human with an average height and looks but with a white screen attached to his chest. If he were left in the middle of a crowd to stand like a non-existent species with his chest being covered, he would never be identified as a robot. His face seemed as human as I am. His body parts were new and shiny. I walked straight to Honey's bedroom, opened his locker with a code mentioned in those papers. I found a chip and knew immediately what to do. Soon the robot made a machinery noise so loud that the morning birds flew away in an instant. I waited for ten minutes and then saw something on his chest that I fell back at once. My eyes moved as fast as they could from left to right and top to bottom while they read, "Hello Kara Darim."

No word was uttered but I could hear my name being called with hundred and forty decibels passing through my auditory nerves. The machine sound interrupted once again while the robot made a greeting gesture with his right-hand standing firmly in the air. My heart raced, hands became cold, and a shiver ran up my spine. "You don't have to name me. I am Quip 713," appeared on his chest. As a reflex, I turned off the switch located behind his head and then he just laid still as though in deep sleep. I justified my actions with an instruction I suddenly remembered, "Switch off your brain for at least eight hours a day at all costs." I wondered how he knew my name, but I thought he was programmed that way since Honey knew only I would activate Quip 713. But as dangerous as it may sound, very soon I realized that I was completely wrong. Would you all believe me if I say Quip 713 has a brain of his own?" I asked and paused. Murmur arose from all corners of the room.

"Yes, Quip 713 was a living and thinking robot," I added. Some laughed, some thought I was bluffing or had become a lunatic, some stood up and left the room, but some believed in me. And so, I continued to speak. "I tested his brain at my lab in secrecy, keeping his head switch on and found such surprising facts, that I just couldn't believe myself. I saw a living brain inside his metal skull when I ran the tests. Quip 713 had a brain with functioning cognition just like a human's but ten times faster and smarter. I tried to perform some more tests on my subject and suddenly his chest blinked, 'I feel the pain that you cannot believe my existence, Mrs. Kara Darim. Your husband was quite unlike you.' What can you expect? I froze and passed out in a moment. I believe it took me fifty hours to open my eyes. As soon as I gained consciousness, I saw Quip 713 standing straight at a distance, with his chest screen brighter than ever, emitting a circular pattern of rays. I couldn't stand the energy band. With closed eyes, I dragged myself towards him to cover the screen with my hand. I just couldn't believe that was the portal, that was where it all began!"

I could hear from the audience, "Why?", "What happened?", "What do you mean by a portal?", "Do you think you're talking sense?". I simply continued without any bother. "I was successful in my attempt, but suddenly felt a strange silence in the atmosphere. My contracted eyes dilated at once and tears rolled out to reach my chin. With a horrific expression, I saw a hundred thousand screens flashed at once, "Hello Kara Darim" and you would never know how I screamed till my vocal cords needed rest." I took a long pause and said, "Their world was muted, yet so busy in mind, just the same way you are now." No one in the room said anything. Nobody moved as well. So, I went on without any further delay. "Welcome to a new world" appeared on the screen of Quip 713.

What I saw was a new world indeed. I was alone in a far-off world, if I may say so, inhabited by living robots who looked just like humans possessing their consciousness. 'We have copied biological brains from our ancestors, scanned and uploaded into our metallic bodies produced by Father Robots. Our brains were made to advance cognitively with every generation now,' I read on his chest. I didn't grasp what he meant but it did not work vice-versa." Everyone in the room burst out laughing. "Yes, I felt dumb literally and metaphorically. I thought silently for myself that not switching off his head button for two continuous days might have opened a portal for his super brain cells to connect to his world. But why in the first place was Quip 713 on our planet? Did Honey know about a parallel universe like this already? With such terrifying thoughts and a face, I walked slowly in a direction I did not know, looked up and saw a sun-set sky with robots flying here and there.

Kara, how did you even come here? Was it meant to be? Is this even a reality? Am I never going back to study a normal human being again? Is this how your life's going to end? Will Quip 713 and his like attack me? Am I really in a far-off world? Broon, Honey, I have lots to tell and yell at you. Kara! Kara! With such thoughts, my mind fell asleep. I woke up with a raced heartbeat, felt I was still alive and decided to explore what is right in front of me. Busy streets with shops and groceries, food and machinery, labs and museums, everything was so like things in a world I used to live except that here, the technology felt extra-terrestrial. These species' brains could connect from anywhere to anyone in an instant and talk through their chest screens. I saw 'The Robot Generation Laboratory'. Honey must be working here, I said and smiled in despair. It seemed like every robot knew I was coming and so they didn't bother my presence. Everyone in that place was so busy with their own lives. Perhaps, it was their kind of New York or Tokyo.

Just then, I sensed a robot's hand on my shoulder and turned behind in terror. "Honey, sorry but I am here,' appeared on the chest screen. Continuous pairs of shock waves in my head were felt again and I started to cry out like a child in fear. "Broon Darim 238" kept blinking on the screen. This time it was the best reason to pass out again, but I had regained my consciousness and stood still like a frozen tree. "I learned about a parallel universe inhabited by advanced living human robots during my research experiments. One afternoon, the portal opened, and I landed here unexpectedly while I was dead there right in front of you. I want to belong to this place now. I hope there comes a time when every living species could choose where they wanted to live," appeared brightly on Darim's chest. I almost heard his voice through the screen clearly and confidently. I remember how I responded to him that day", I said to the audience with a grin on my face.

"Mr. Broon Darim 238, if my husband were a robot, I am willing to live with him but from a place where I feel I belong to", I said. The air was filled with warmth and sweetness while we laughed together once again. I felt much better in my mind and body at that very moment. I touched his white screen again while it emitted the same circular pattern of rays and to my surprise, I found myself back at my lab along with Quip 713. "I want to live here", appeared on his chest." I smiled at the audience and asked, "So what about you? Do you want to start over somewhere else?" and perhaps, they gave it a thought too as all heads turned towards Quip 713.

14

MY REALITY

BY BIBIN K BABU

Consciousness, a state of awareness of oneself and the world. Scope of this definition is one that surpasses one's reality.

Scientists have made progress in many fields but have stagnated for decades in understanding the origin of life.

Darwin's theory does provide a hierarchical explanation to life as we know it but is limited to the origin of a primordial soup.

What caused life and where does one derive his consciousness is still a mystery.

The universe as we know it could be nothing, but an illusion created by our mind not at the concrete level but in the quantum realm scientists have found that particles react relatively to one's will or consciousness.

30th December 2019

Patient Name: Edward Lane

Occupation: Tenor Soloist

Recording 1

Dr Albino enters the cabin, he was a man in his 60s who has a profound experience in human psychology and psychiatry, he holds a PhD in the same. He had a well-combed yet grizzly hair with signs of wrinkles appearing on his cheeks.

He hung his coat and settled down. He gave a quick eye behind to check whether his assistant was ready to record the session.

"So Mr. Edward, after a long wait of 2 months I'm happy to see you, actually I'm excited and intrigued to listen to your story, which no doubt will inspire thousands of our next generations. So where do you wanna start!"

Edward took a long breath staring at the ceiling reminiscing his past.

"To be accurate it started in my early twenties, but it hit me exactly a year ago. It was 31st December 2018 New Year's Eve at the city of Manhattan, there where thousands chanting my name in their peak voices, they all had their hands up waving in unison, for them I was an orphan kid who dropped out of his education, who left his orphanage before attaining legal maturity to pursue his ambition. For them, I was the one who conquered the steps of success one by one to reach here, to deliver his best and biggest performance till date, and I Did. But they didn't know." Edward grabs a bottle of water by the desk and gulps a few.

"They didn't know that the person who was their inspiration was trembling, I was holding my mic stand with both my arms to keep myself steady, I held the mic stand strong to stop the shiver, my pupils were dilated, and my mouth was feeling dry. I tried keeping a wry smile to the audience till the curtain closed and once it did, I collapsed.

I was having a seizure and had to be carried to my cabin, they gave glucose and other treatments once I stopped seizing, but I knew those didn't matter, what mattered to me was in my bottom desk drawer.

I signalled my assistant to empty the room and close the door.

Just as the doors were shut, I crawled through the floor, reached out to the syringe and injected a chuck load of meth to my veins.

Everything began to settle; my breathing became normal and now had a clear vision.

That was me, the conceited bastard who aimed supremacy was a desperate drug addict."

"Yash, could you please pause the camera for a second. (Dr Albino signalled his assistant)

Mr. Edward do you want to record all this, once out it could endanger your entire career."

"Every human has a shadow within, and his life's purpose is said to be fulfilled when he conquers them. This is my story where I finally conquer my shadow and I want the world to know it."

"2nd January i.e., two days after my performance at Manhattan.

I was driving, on my way from Nebraska to New York, I received a call from Julie (my assistant) saying there was a surprise raid in my bungalow in suspicion of possession of drugs and they've confiscated the entire stuff.

She wanted me to stay out of New York for a while till my manager found a way to get me out and suppress the media's attention. I suspected Johnny to be behind this and soon enough Julie clarified it. Johnny was the sponsor of the new year's gig and was a fan of mine but couldn't bear the fact that his ardent role model was a drug addict. It devastated him, we even had quite a scene in the hallway in regard to my abuse.

I was furious at him, I dialled him up immediately to give him something to remember, but the situation turned upside down when I lost control of my driving during the fury which resulted in a car crash.

Reports were stating that my car had tumbled twice before hitting a pole to stop. I couldn't remember any of these, the next thing I remember was waking up in Passedina city hospital two days later. For some reason, my arms and legs were strapped to my bed like I was mentally unstable. On inquiry, I found that I hadn't been cooperative for the last couple of days which resulted in a broken arm of one of the nurses.

But none of that mattered to me. I was hungry and was craving, not for food but some meth.

All my stuff was seized, and the inspectors needed a little more than a few dollars to negotiate but the deal didn't include returning my stuff.

Before too long I started losing my senses, my throat and lips started to swell, my vision was getting yellowish and there was a constant ringing noise in my ear.

There was a doctor in my room checking through my reports. I was persuasive when it would come to drugs and 5000 dollars did me the trick this time. He offered to give me some alternative drug which was banned by the government as it induced methamphetamine like high to one's brain. The drug was supposedly made to cure depression and other psychological ailments, but the research was now shut and only a few were left in the restricted section.

He offered to get me a few 10mls of that which was more

that I could bargain for.

I was so desperate that I injected myself with a couple of those 10mls in the first try and that's all I remember."

"So, it was after that dosage everything began?" Dr. Albino enquired curiously.

"Yes", Edward took another long breath.

"I felt a gush of chilly wind to my forehead, I didn't sense it then but when I heard a noise from somewhere my eyes struck open to a completely unfamiliar environment. I was in a bed wearing someone's pajamas. I gently got down in amazement to something different.

I heard chirping birds, quacking ducks and dancing trees. It all felt different yet soothing. I kept hearing the noise from before, it was a woman calling out to someone 'Alphonse... Alphonse' it said. I started walking towards a window beside me and opened the screen.

Rays blocked my eyesight but when it cleared, I could see.

The scenic beauty of nature, there was a huge farm with many domestic animals and different types of feathered friends.

I felt a pat on my head.

'Couldn't you answer? I've been yelling for some time now.' A woman spoke to me as though I was someone close to her.

'Here take these clothes to big brother and have them dry cleaned by tomorrow' she handed a pile of clothes in a bag to me and left-back in a hurry.

I was numbed for a while trying to contemplate what was happening.

'Ahoy,' I heard another voice from the backyard.

I looked through the window to see a man in his 50s with a

shovel by his shoulder. He was naked by his torso and had a long piece of cloth wrapped around his legs, he had dirt all over his belly and looked completely exhausted.

'Yo Sleepyhead, get the clothes out fast and get down here, I'd be needing another hand here with me'. Weirdly enough I felt as though he was addressing me, I looked just in case to see if somebody else was here, that was when I saw a small portrait hanging by the wall. My heart started pumping blood at an alarming rate and I started to feel dizzy when I saw a picture of me with the women and man from before and two other young boys as though we were a family.

I took a closer look at the portrait, no doubt it was me.

The palpitation got intense, I thought I was delirious.

I heard it again 'Alphonse', I didn't know what to do. I ran, ran out of the house I could hear them calling me, but I gave a deaf ear and ran, I didn't know where I was running, the streets felt new and the environment felt weird, nevertheless I kept running, I didn't stop till I reached a dead end.

There was a small tavern there, I got in to have something which would relax my mind a little but surprisingly enough everyone there was staring at me like I had broken some sacred covenant, midst the crowd I heard that word again. 'Alphonse'. It sent a shiver down my spine. 'how'd you know I was here?' a small man stood out, I realised soon enough that he was in the portrait. 'Did you come all the way here to hand me the dry-cleaning clothes?' he said staring at my arm. I forgot I had that, with a wry smile I said 'yes' and handed the bag over and ran back. I could hear his voice from behind 'don't tell this to Ma and pa'.

I sat down on a small bench to get the head and tail of what's going on, but it was impossible to comprehend. I understood that the woman and man I saw earlier was supposedly my parents and the guy whom I just saw was my brother, but it didn't change the fact that they never existed before.

A minibus passed by me and something felt familiar, I looked up and it was a convent bus titled 'Lost yet redeemed souls'. It was the orphanage where I grew up.

I signalled the bus to halt and got in so that finally I could meet some familiar faces.

Mother Magdalena gave me a huge hug with joyful tears, I felt a sense of nostalgia when I met her after all these years.

From there I found out that the women, man and guy were my families. Not adopted but my blood, I was lost to them as an infant and after 16 years of search they'd found me in this convent.

I stopped thinking and I stopped trying to understand. At that moment I just wanted to meet my family.

I was dropped back to my home and I just stood at the doorway hesitant to get in, to meet my family which never existed before. Soon enough I saw my mother running towards me, she had tears filled in her eyes and worrisome expressions all over her face. She hugged me tightly like she never wanted to let go, my father stood at a distance with a sense of relief.

I looked at my mom at her beautiful blue eyes and glowing face and said those words which I never thought I could ever say 'm...m... maa'. There was gentle rain which helped me in concealing the tears which never stopped.

I hugged her and wept, wept as if I was a small baby, she gently patted my head and said 'shhh... don't cry, everything will be alright we're all here. Just never leave us again, my soul can't bear to go through what I've been through'. My younger brother ran and hugged me and mother both, my elder brother just returned and saw us, he didn't know what to do so he too hugged us, my father stood at a distance wiping his tears off, I looked at him.' what? I'm not hugging you' he said.

We had a beautiful dinner when I understood how beautiful it is to dine with one's family. This reality made no sense, but this was the one where I wanted to be right now, but life had different plans. A huge bolt of lightning struck, and the power went down and simultaneously I woke up back in the hospital bed."

"So, you mean to say you had an intense long hallucination?" Dr, Albino enquired leaning forward.

"That's what I thought too but after some digging, I found that... (Edward paused for a while) the name Edward was not my original name, it was given to me by Mother Magdalena when she found me lost in the streets of Delaware."

"Which means the fact you were lost in your childhood was true. So do you think maybe even your parents...?"

"Yes, Yes, Her name is Elaine and his name is Jay, turns out he was a native Indian who met my mom here and settled, they had three sons, Mike the eldest one, David the youngest and Alphonse the lost one," Edward said those with sporadic running tears. Albino gave Ed a moment to settle down, "They are now in Austin, Texas. My Dad, Mom and two siblings."

"Wait a minute that would mean that your hallucination was a real one?"

"Have you heard about the theory of multiverse? with every decision you make you create a whole another reality where you chose differently. My decision to become the world's most renowned musician led me here as an irascible drug addict and an alternative where I'd chosen to stay back in the convent gave me a family."

"But that's impossible and radical. We don't have any evidence for the existence of such other universe's." Dr. Albino was completely awestruck.

"Consciousness is a distinct entity than our mind, so Maybe, reality is made up by human consciousness, by one's decisions and the only way to access other reality is through one's consciousness."

"So, you say overdose of that alternative drug caused this?"

"I don't know the science behind all those, but I believe that reality exists only because there is a part within me which wants that. Reality is induced by one's mind, it can be whatever we want, we shape our reality."

"I don't argue against that, and I doubt even our scientists have any argument against that, for all we know consciousness is a mystery which is yet to be solved. By the way what happened next?"

"Soon enough after I woke up, I had a surprise visitor, it was the inspector who did the raid and he gave me only one choice, I had to quit drugs only then he would keep the case from leaking, at that time I felt that he'd read my mind.

The reality from that other universe made me realize what I was longing for, it was neither fame nor stardom, it was being considered. But my ego had superseded my desire.

Anyways with the help of the inspector I got into a rehabilitation center, he even helped me find my family, it took me 8 months to completely get rid of all the toxins within me and another 2 months to get me back on my feet."

"So that's how you conquered your shadow. Impressive!" Dr. Albino leaned back, he gently gave a tap to the armrest and got up, he took his coat back and signaled his assistant to turn the camera off and pack it up, he left the office but swiftly returned.

"I'm sorry but I can't help but ask, Why? I mean why me? What is your motive behind this session? What do you plan to do?"

"I want the world to know what kind of a man I was and what kind of a man I became and the only sure way to get their assurance is when the final session is done before a professional."

"What are you planning?"

"World's biggest music concert, I'm going to arrange one in Copacabana tomorrow and beat the previous one, but when I do that, I don't want the audience to be there with an illusion of who I was in the past and I want them to be there after knowing who I'm right now, that's the reason I wanted this session published to the entire news channel and social media."

"What if they don't turn up?"

31st December 2019 New Year's Eve, Copacabana

I kept on asking myself that question over and over as I was backstage of what could be the world's biggest music concert.

This was the first time I was performing without a load of meth inside me, today I understood what real nervousness was, facing such a large crowd with all the attention on myself, it gave me a chilly shiver.

I quickly took my phone and rang Julie.

"Are they here?"

"Yes, sir seat no.."

"No that's not required."

I hung up and calmed myself down.

"It is my first performance in front of my family and I'm not going to mess it up," I said to myself.

First time in my life I looked up and gave glory for what I have today and got on to the stage.

I was not nervous now because the reality I was facing right now is the one I made myself and I am going to proudly face it with a straight head.

15

SENTIENT BEINGS

BY NIKITA K

R iya was sitting on her balcony with her morning coffee and the newspaper on her iPad. It was not a particularly bright day, neither did it seem like it was going to rain. It was neutral and colourless, much like everything else in her life nowadays.

"So, what are your plans for today?" Neal had walked in.

"Oh, I don't know, same as usual, I guess. I'm supposed to meet Lee after work."

"You seem off nowadays, like you're not happy about anything."

"Really? What do I have to be unhappy about? Everything's perfect."

"Maybe not unhappy, sort of a perpetual state of boredom."

She was quiet.

"Why do you have to look so perfect every day?" she asked in an attempt of deflection.

She could never get used to being around Neal. It was as if someone had designed him to perfection with a blueprint from her dreams. A lean build, wavy jet-black hair, jawbones that could cut diamonds, and piercing grey eyes, they always looked like they were peering into her soul and way beyond that. The intensity of his gaze was alleviated only by his smile. She kissed him goodbye and left for work.

Neal knew he was right; he was worried about her. She was not always like this. When they had met, Riya used to be in love with life itself. She used to talk about her dreams and aspirations, what she likes and dislikes, what she loves. They used to keep exploring new things to do, life used to be an adventure when he was with Riya. He was not sure when this started changing. Initially, it felt as if they were just another couple moving on to the next phase in their relationship. But now, he was not so sure anymore. He was out of ideas, Riya never looked interested in anything anymore, she was always in search of something intangible and constantly dissatisfied with everything at hand.

There was hardly anyone in the office that day. Riya had to test her software on the new robots in the factory, she needed to be present on site.

"When did you get here?" Aisha was in the office.

"A while ago. Do you know where everyone else is? The office is deserted today."

"Some of them are around. The work has been sparse lately. So, a lot of them are working from home."

"Well can you find me some people? You can join too."

"Sure, I'll let everyone know. Also, what do you think of the latest robots? They're brilliant, aren't they?"

"Yes, Aisha you look brilliant. Now can you please load this patch and help me out?"

"Why are you so grim? I thought we're friends, you can talk to me you know. Things aren't good with Neal?", as Riya started loading her program.

"Of course, we are. But there is nothing substantial, Neal is great, I don't know what it is. I've just been feeling like there is no novelty left in living anymore."

"From all the time I have known you, I'm sure you'll figure it out".

"Thanks, you're too sweet".

"Please select personality traits. You can also choose a custom set", Aisha said.

Riya clicked on the custom option.

"Enter the name."

Aisha.

"Hello Riya, how are you? When did you get here? It's been long".

"Hey there Aisha. Now let's check out the latest features."

It was evening by the time Riya got done with her work. The sky was a mix of bright purple and orange. Unlike morning, the pageantry of colours only seemed to be contrasting her life, making the banality even more obvious. She had already received the clearance to meet Leena. Soon she slipped into her hazmat suit and headed on to their Rooftop cafe. Leena was wearing a mild orange hazmat suit herself.

"Nice suit", Riya said.

"I know right? Jay designed it for me."

"So, how's work? How are things with Jay?"

"Oh, you know work is the same as always. Combine the DNA, tissue regeneration, create babies, send them off to be raised. Jay is away to get his monthly system updates"

"Wow, they took the fun out of making babies, didn't they?"

"C'mon it's not that grim. In fact, thanks to your work we still get to have fun, without the threat of having kids."

It had been a while since Riya had laughed like that.

"What's wrong Ri? You seem different today."

"I don't know, I'm bored I guess."

"Bored with what? Having the perfect guy, perfect job, and perfect life?"

"Well yes, is it that ridiculous if I was? This stupid virus has taken away everything unpredictable about our lives and left us with perfection and predictability. What if I didn't mind the imperfections and liked the unpredictability? What if I don't want to be with a guy who can read my blood pressure and my heartbeats, and understands every minute change in my demeanour? What if I want someone with real emotions? You're the only human I've met in what feels like a lifetime. Is it that weird if I miss those self-obsessed and arrogant guys from before? At least they had their dreams and aspirations. Now I'm bored and tired and I wish I could hug you without these designer hazmat suits."

Leena was looking at her as if she had just spoken another language.

"Okay, I'll stop whining. I do really like Neal. I cannot think of a single bad quality in him." Riya said as she realized her best friend did not share her real opinion.

It was a luxury just to be sitting this close to any human in the first place. Both Riya and Leena had lived in the old times when the humans did not have to wear hazmat suits, nor did they have to get clearance to meet each other. Fashion used to be about the clothes and not the hazmat suits. They had relationships with other humans and not robots. It felt like a dream as Riya was having her coffee through the sanitized straw in her suit. It did not help that Leena seemed to have forgotten it altogether, she had adjusted effortlessly.

The virus had left about one million humans in the world, and even with all the scientific developments, there was no cure. It was found easier to simply create a civilization of sentient robots that would keep the humans safe from each other. Being anywhere within 50 meters of another human required clearance and a hazmat suit. The virus could sense life and get activated otherwise.

The animals and plants were still safe, the ecosystems had thrived with the onset of the virus. The planet was recovering marvellously from all the damage humans had inflicted over centuries. Crime rates were negligible since there were plenty of resources for the sparse population.

Riya took off her suit as she was out of the 50-meter radius. Her car was synced with Neal, so he knew she's on her way back.

"Hey, I have computed a few different personalities for you today. I thought you were bored with me in the morning. Do you want to try them out?" Neal had genuine concern in his eyes. It was very easy to forget it was programmed, he had more human reflexes than most humans.

"Oh dear, it wasn't you, I was bored of." She kissed him as she cancelled the new options.

"You can increase my humour setting or try the adventurous one."

Riya rolled her eyes.

"Yes, honey I know, I programmed you myself, remember? Let's make dinner."

Next morning smelled of waffles and coffee.

"What's the occasion?" Riya a sked as she hugged him from

the back.

"Nothing, I just felt like it. How do you feel about hiking today?"

"Sounds great, you checked for its schedule?" as she had the waffle straight from the waffle iron.

"Yep, there's only one human booked to go there today, that too in the evening. I have made our booking until 6 PM."

"Well then what are we waiting for?"

Hiking was a much-needed change. They had packed a bottle of wine and food; he was carrying everything in his bag. He could not take a swim in the lake with her, he was not waterproof yet, he chose to take her pictures and set up the picnic instead. That is when an alarm suddenly started ringing.

"It is a warning alert! I'm scanning the area for another human" he shouted.

Riya got out of the water and got dressed. There was a thick cover of trees all around them, no human in sight.

"I've found him, he's around 100 meters away. I'm reporting him to the authorities, he's here without clearance. Both of you are in danger."

"It's alright, maybe he just wanted some fresh air, we'll just tell him to maintain the distance."

"If you say so, I'll go and have a word."

It turned out that the other human had found a loophole to escape from the distance monitoring and he had been coming to the lake for some fresh air for a while. He had no idea that there was someone else around that day. The virus was activated as soon as any two humans were within 50 meters of each other, they could have both died that day. Riya wondered if that human had the same thoughts as her. If this was his way of defying the system. She wanted to go and meet him, maybe he had trouble adjusting to the system just like her. However, Neal was designed to keep her from any other human at any cost, it was impossible.

"How did that other human seem, when you went to meet him?" she said on their way back.

"What do you mean? He was alright, just an average human. He sure scared me for a bit though, when the alarm went off"

"Did he look happy? Or content?"

"I'm not sure"

"I see," there was no way to find out if there was anyone else. Loneliness seemed to be gnawing at everything in its way, no amount of perfect human-like robots could have filled the void.

"Alright, what are we going to do for dinner, I'm too tired to cook", even with a low battery, he looked just as flawless as ever.

"You've done enough, I'll cook today."

"That means we'll have to order in," there was no need to increase his humour setting after all.

Neal looked like he could fall asleep at any moment after dinner. It seemed he had spent a lot of energy. She was tired too. She plugged him into the sleep mode next to her as she got into the bed.

He woke up the next morning in a pool of blood. The horror of what had happened dawned on him and he knew he had to turn and see for himself. But he couldn't. It was as if his neck was jammed from turning. He got out of the bed, and there she was, with a gun in her hand, and a gunshot wound through her forehead. He was covered in blood himself. He instinctively screamed, he tried to revive her, he could tell she was different, but she had not programmed the protocol to deal with human mortality into him. He started crying, he called the hospital, he had no idea how to function anymore. When the paramedics rushed in, they found a robot that was disintegrating into spare parts, like a fish taken out of water.

They were never able to recover him, some of the parts had melted into each other, while some were completely burnt. There were bits and pieces left, which didn't make any sense.

"A human would have moved on to someone else, not broken down like this, let's report this defect", they said while disposing of what was left.

16

A TALE OF TIMELESS LOVE

BY PRAVALLIKA KADIRI

ANIKA

The alarm rings for the 5th time.

"Damn! I'm late again! Why does it always happen to me? Rush Anika, get yourself out of the house in the next 10 minutes." I yelled at myself.

How else would I expect myself to wake up after so much partying last night? The party was too much fun! I can't believe Mr. Handsome was there too. Before I started rushing into the thoughts about him, I pushed myself out of the bed, leaving the bed undone as always, I rushed to the bathroom to have a 5minute shower, wore a blue jean paired with a white shirt and a messy bun with red lipstick. That is always my go-to look when I have no time, that is almost every other day. Whereas, on the days when I have a lot of time to get ready, I put on a jumpsuit or a solid-coloured dress with my hair straightened and a nude lipstick for my lips. On those days I see Mr. Handsome staring at me more often than he usually does. And he just starts looking elsewhere when I catch him doing that. Man! I love that feeling! I wonder why he is so reserved, he doesn't drink, doesn't dance yet comes to the party! Ugh, he is so not Anika's type, but why do I get so attracted to him? Maybe Rebecca ma'am was right about opposite poles getting attracted, never understood that in school though!

I diverted myself as I grabbed a bite of my sandwich and got out of my house to work, it wasn't in 10 minutes though!

MOHAK

What a beautiful morning! This chai, the book, some music, and her thoughts in between.

I couldn't resist myself from thinking about her. The way she talks, dances, eats, walks, especially on the days when she dresses prettier than usual. Last night her beauty knew no bounds! She wore a glittery dress, party appropriate. Her face was a lot shinier than her glittery dress.

"Hmm... Good decision Mohak! You would have missed it if you wouldn't have gone to the party," I appreciate myself as I get ready to go to work.

I work at GRP Consultancy, which is in the hi-tech city, so I was all ready to hit the traffic an hour before my office timings. The traffic would be immense, but all the stress would vanish once I looked at her in the office.

ANIKA

I reached the office, but I stood near the stairs and called Rithika who is my bro friend [a best friend who is like a bro].

"Bro, the boss isn't here, you can come up", she says right after she lifts the call.

Once I entered, I saw everyone planning stuff for the trip tomorrow to Lushai Hills in Mizoram. I see Mr. Handsome and he looks at me, smiles, and blinks his eyes. He doesn't do that with everyone, and I know it. Meanwhile, Rithika comes and pulls me aside.

"Bro, are you sure you are going to propose to him on the trip?" she asks me.

"Of course, Rithu! I waited too long, and I have to do it now. Everything has to be perfect as we planned, near the mountains with a beautiful view!"

"Yeah, I'll look at that, don't worry," she said.

Later that day I took half a day off to get back home and started packing for the trip.

MOHAK

The next morning,

All of us boarded a flight to Mizoram. And I was searching for my seat number and I saw her sitting on the seat right next to me.

How else could I get luckier? We have spoken a lot of times, but never like this! Sitting right next to each other on a 6-hour long flight, somewhere among the clouds!

"So, how come you are early today?" I asked and tried to start a conversation.

"Yesterday wasn't a party day and today is a trip day, how could I be late?" she said.

"Yeah, that's right. So, have you been to Mizoram before?", I asked because I just didn't want an awkward silence between us.

"Nope, I haven't", she said.

I felt that the conversation was getting too boring, so I

decided to make it interesting and funny.

So...I randomly started this:

"KNOCK KNOCK"

This is the first thing that comes into my mind when I think of the word funny! Don't judge my level of being humourous though, hands-down I am bad with jokes or interesting conversations.

"Who's there?" she replies.

"Oman"

"Oman who?"

"Oman... You... you are cute!" I said.

"Oh god! Stop it", she says as she blushes. She looked even cuter then.

Inner me – wohhhhhooooo my lame ass joke worked! Dude, you aren't that bad at this! Keep on going!

So, I continued the knock-knock jokes, flirted with her, laughed a lot, watched her blushing the whole time and it was me who just kept talking the whole time which is so unlike me!

It was a long flight, so we slept after a few knock-knock jokes.

ANIKA

Finally, we were done with our 6-hour long flight and I couldn't wait to tell Rithu about everything that we spoke.

We had to take a bus to reach our Resort near Lushai Hills and it was a 5-hour Journey.

I got into the bus, I ran and sat beside Rithu, she knew I would now eat her brain, but she was excited too.

"So how was it brooo?" she asked with a bunch of excitement.

"Bro, good that we managed to take Arvind's seat somehow, I sat right next to him and we spoke so much and laughed like nothing else, he is not as reserved as he looks, I Mean when he is with me!!"

"I always knew that he is a different person when you are around him. Now, tell me what you guys talked about? Anything sexy Ahhh?" She teases me.

"No bro, it was all about knock-knock jokes and damn we laughed so hard" I said with a smile brighter than the sun.

"What? You guys were on a 6-hour flight and all you both spoke about was knock-knock jokes! You guys will probably make the weirdest pair in the whole world!" she said.

"Huh, you just jealous bitch."

"Oh yeah, jealous of; knock-knock... Who is there... a jealous bitch!" she said.

Both of us started laughing and then we spoke about my proposal plan.

MOHAK

We finally reached our Resort after the longest journey ever, all of us were too tired, so everyone went to their rooms to sleep and I rushed towards the manager of the Resort to ask for a beautiful proposal set up around that place, near a scenic spot to propose. It had mountains with greenery and a huge waterfall right in front. All I wanted was to propose to her and then to have a candlelight dinner, and a walk on those long roads covered by the branches of the trees on either side of the road, probably talking about our future or maybe knock-knock jokes (we never know), I could not wait for that to happen! I always dreamt of proposing to her someday and I felt nothing could be better than this place, between the most beautiful breathtaking views. Yes, I am going to propose to her, though we are going to stay here for 3 days, tomorrow is going to be the big day!

The Manager said that he'll set up everything as per my instructions, so everything was ready and now I needed to prepare a proposal speech, but I didn't want to because I wanted it to be a spontaneous and a heartfelt one.

So, I freshened up and got to bed all excited for the big day of our lives.

ANIKA

After we reached the resort, everyone wanted to sleep, but I just wanted to roam around that magnificent place, I felt that I belonged there, between those mountains with that fresh breeze, so I asked Rithu if she wanted to come along with me for a walk. She refused at first, but I took her anyway. Meanwhile, my other friend Esha wanted to join us too.

It was around 7.30 in the evening, quite dark and three of us went for a walk. We walked and walked, the road was quite a good half the way, but it started getting bumpy, rutted and uneven.

"Bro, let's go back, the road is getting worse, it's like we've come for a trek and to walk." Rithu said.

Just then we heard a waterfall, I got so excited, the sound was a dense one like someone wanted to scare the shit out of us.

I wanted to see where the sound was coming from, Rithu and Esha stayed there because they were tired of that bumpy walk, but I walked more forward and damn that was the end of the cliff and all I could see in front of me was a beautiful waterfall, between the humongous mountains and a very rapid

Water flow below, it was dark but the sound got me goosebumps.

"Bro look at this here... It looks like a Baahubali waterfall...so beautiful...come here guys," I said and turned behind to walk towards them, but my left leg had different plans, it slips off and I lost my balance and I floated in the air, like how the heroine of baahubali does in one of the songs, but she knew where to land unlike me! I couldn't sense myself. At first, I could hear Rithu shouting "ANIKAAAAAA." Later, it was so windy that my hearing got blocked and my lungs were dying to get some normal air instead of the harsh wind. I tried to wriggle my hands as if that would get me back to the cliff. I couldn't see anything and now I know why I felt like I belonged there. Before I could think of anything else I fell into that dense water and it was all blank..blank and just blank, I could feel some force, very harsh as if someone was trying to steal my soul from me but later I stopped feeling that force too.

I opened my eyes, I was all drenched in water, lying down on a rock, the sky was like a galaxy, it had a different colour like that of a purplish white. I got up and looked around, there was water flowing besides, the surroundings were too bizarre, I could find no one, the trees and the atmosphere there was also strange, everything felt very unusual.

What is this? Where am I? Is this where people come when they die? Am I dead? Am I not going to see any of my people now? What about Mohak? All these questions were racing in my mind.

I was too puzzled to even shed a tear. I barely knew where I was and what I was doing there. Just then I saw a guy walking outside from a tunnel-like thing. He was not dressed up like a normal human for sure!

I went into the tunnel and there was a path, I didn't know where that path was leading to but I walked anyway. I continued walking for a while and then I saw a different place altogether, where people were moving around normally but all of them dressed strangely. Just like the man I saw before. All of them looked like normal humans, they had families, people there were eating some weird food! All of them were talking in some other language that I've never heard before. Nothing there was normal, everything around me was surreal, I was the only odd person out there and people were staring at me as if I was an alien.

"If this is where people come after they die, there must be different kinds of people, but all these people here follow the same things [like their language and dressing style]", I thought.

So, I knew that something was wrong, but I didn't know what was?

The sky was a little too peculiar. I didn't know which part of the day it was, I wanted to go back, back to my people, to my Mohak. I saw a spot to sit and I sat there thinking of what to do and about what was happening. I could see couples in love, a mother kissing her daughter, a son fighting with his dad, old people playing with their grandkids...I could see love. The strangest place, but the same love! I slept there for a long time and I spent many hours wandering around and just sleeping. I ate nothing all that time. I was missing Mohak, I wanted to look at him, at least for one last time and tell him what I always felt for him. I cried my eyes out. I wished Mohak could be there with me.

Just then I walked into a forest kinda place where I saw a crowd surrounding something, I went there to see and all I saw was Mohak! Lying down lifeless! Dead! Yes, it was Mohak, he must have come searching for me and he has died! I didn't have the guts to go close to him and I ran away from there, I kept running, running from the pain and the guilt. I couldn't take the fact that my Mohak was lying dead because of me!

I stopped near a tree because I could hardly breathe as I was panting a lot, just then I saw a silhouette of a man sitting on a rock, he felt quite familiar to me, so I went closer to him and he turned his face, and it was Mohak.

"I couldn't believe my eyes, I just saw Mohak dead!"

Mohak came running towards me, hugged me and cried like he has received a Nobel prize, but I couldn't hug him back, all that I was thinking about was dead Mohak and just then I realized that the dead person was in those strange clothes and this Mohak was wearing normal ones, like how we usually wear. I realized that the dead person resembled Mohak, but it wasn't him. My Mohak was right in front of me so I hugged him back and both of us couldn't hold our happiness.

"I came for you all the way and you know how it feels like to find you? Like I'm reliving my life again!" he said.

And the next thing that happened was..

Mohak went on his knees and he said:

"We are on a rock by the water, mountains and trees all around, the purple sky, the galaxy above, the stars shining like they are blessing us and all I want to say here is KNOCK KNOCK."

"Who is there, I replied.

"Value"

"Value who?", I said.

"Value be the love of my life by always staying there by my side without falling off a cliff or falling into the water, by coping up with my knock-knock jokes until my last joke, by letting me fall for you more and more with every day passing by?"

"Yes, I will!", I said laughing and crying out of happiness and then I bent on my knees and we kissed each other. Our first kiss was destined to happen somewhere in a different universe, under a purple sky and the galaxies but with the same love. "How did you even land here out of nowhere Mohak?", I asked him after some time.

And he explained to me everything which left me startled.

MOHAK

Two days ago...

Around 8.00 pm Rithu called me and explained what had happened and I rushed to that spot. We searched for her everywhere around but couldn't find her anywhere. We called the cops, and they searched all the nearby places too. Everyone assumed that she died, but I never accepted that because we didn't find her body and my heart knew that she was alive! While searching for her, I got to know that the waterfall and the water flow below has always been a mysterious thing, there are rumours that people disappear from there. If it were true, she'd be alive somewhere! So, I finally decided to jump off the same cliff, just like how she fell. I didn't know where it would take me if I'd be dead or alive if I'd find her or not but none of this stopped me. I didn't want to miss a single chance of knowing where she was. So, I jumped. I fell into the water and the next thing I know is I am in some strange place.

I hoped that she was there, I roamed around for hours and I sat on a rock and just then she appeared in front of me!!!

ANIKA

"How could you do that Mohak? You'd have been dead!!", I

yelled. "But I'm not, we found each other, found our love! Worth taking that risk, right?"

"Yeah, right, I love you, but what do we do now?", I asked.

"We should get back to our world, this is not where we belong. It is going to be risky again, but it might be worth taking that risk. So, are you ready?

"Yes, let's go!"

We went to that place exactly where we first opened our eyes in that strange universe. There was water flow, rapid enough, we knew that we had to fall into it, risking our lives but we had to do it anyway. We looked at each other and kissed, maybe for one last time and we fell into the water and it was all blank again.

I opened my eyes and yes, I was back, back to the blue sky, familiar atmosphere, and the normal world with my Mr. Handsome right next to me! I woke him up and the first thing he said was "worth the risk, isn't it?"

And there we were, all drenched in water, after travelling to a different universe, finding our lost love and returning to the normal world.

This journey had a meaning to it! I saw a doppelganger of Mohak! How crazy is that!

But most importantly, I lived my life in two different universes with different versions of their own and the only thing that was the same is LOVE. However bizarre that universe was, love remained the same and will probably be the same in any other universe too.

After all that roller coaster ride, I realized that be it this universe or the parallel, love finds its way.

17

EARTH 0.02

BY RASAGYA GADE

How are you, my dear?" "Do not be sad." "Should I help you?" said a voice. Max, a 14-year-old boy, who was crying in his room didn't understand where the voice was coming from. More and more questions were being asked. He started crying, even more, thinking there was a ghost in his room. Then, Tom, his dog started turning into fire. Max couldn't understand what was happening. "Don't fear dear, I am Rex, I have always admired you looking into the mirror, in the day and night," said Tom who was a dog. Max couldn't bring himself together for a minute and started splashing water at Tom aka Rex. Rex started laughing and turned himself into Tom and started explaining who he was and where he was from. Max didn't believe what was told to him. Boom!!!!! went to the bed flying in the air.

Max was told that Rex was an alien and could see Max from his mirror as Max's mirror was the twin brother of Rex's mirror. "Hello Max, I am Rin," said another voice. The voice was now the mirror's voice. Max started yelling, "Who are you, why do you want to kill me?" Rex then told him he was from the parallel universe and told him not to worry. Max slowly started to get himself together and started listening to what Rex told. Rex shouted "Kin!!!", and Kin, the bed flew into the room through the window and took the three of them to the Banyan tree. "Max the great" yelled Rex and the tree split open into two and welcomed them into a whole new world. Max could see a pillow, a video game console and many more things walking and flying.

All the four reached Rex's house which was in the exact place where Max's house was. Then Rex told Max not to worry and started explaining what was going on. "This is the Riyo planet and the most developed planet in our universe. I once bought a "the risque mirror" which will help people to make new friends from different planets and universes. I found you from the mirror and thought to meet you, but as soon as I reached your house, I understood that the people on the earth do not know anything about these mirrors and how to use them, so I turned into a dog and reached you. But then I understood that you are a very smart and intelligent guy but you were always betrayed by your friends and your stepmother doesn't take proper care of you. I knew you were going to murder yourself for facing all the difficulties. I know you changed many lives and helped others and was always betrayed."

"You are right Tom, sorry....Rex, I helped many poor people and the bullied people but as I am a black I was never treated the same way the others were treated and I always had you as my only friend Rex, but now that I know there were many aliens in my room..." Rex intervened and said I understand you but I just want to show you the beauty of life and make you understand how beautiful you are from the inside. Rex then explained that Kin was his wife and Rin was his best bud and then took Max to the most beautiful places and made him relax and told him to always work hard as he did and to enjoy every minute and not to care about the bullies and wait for the success.

Max then started questioning "Why are you shaped like a fire? Why did you want to help me? how do you think the 'the risque mirror' reached me?"

"Max, the creatures on this planet are just as humans but as the trends changed, we liked to change ourselves into things and also remember, the right things will reach you at the right time, you should always be patient. Max, it is time to send you back to your planet" said Rex. "I spent 1 month here; my mother will murder me" cried Max. "Do not worry Max, I will take you to the same day that I brought you here."

"I do not know how to thank you, Rex, thank you so much for the help. You helped me understand who I truly am".

"Do not mention that" winked Rex.

"I am going to miss you so much," said Max and left for his planet through the banyan tree.

"THE END," said Max to his son closing the storybook. Max then told his son, Sean, that Rex was none other than Max himself who came from the Future earth/earth - 0.01, the parallel universe which was 20 years ahead of them.

Sean then asked, "why did you lie to your past self-dad?"

Max told him that "he didn't have many friends and was always bullied, and he wanted to change the way he lived. And as soon as my future self-found about our planet, he made all the illusions and made me believe that first, he was a dog and then the fireman and his wife and son were a bed and mirror, respectively. What must be understood is that what you do today will help you become what you are tomorrow, so always think what you are doing is right or wrong and do not care about the bullies."

Sean then continued "Yes dad, you are right and that is why you are so successful and ended racism and helped many people by providing them education and also one should always make good friends like Rin uncle who can support you when you are down, am I right dad?"

Max then replied, "Yes Sean you are right and now it is my time to go to the earth - 0.03 and boost myself up."

18

GATEWAY FROM REAL TO REEL WORLD

BY TUSHAR DUDHADE

Introduction

The phone was ringing for a few seconds now. Roy was on the balcony with the cigarette and coffee mug in his hand. It's been while he'd had his me time. Whenever there is smudge caused by the dark clouds in his Life, he always lights his cigarette and with his favourite wine poured in his favourite glass, he drinks Wine with the drags of his cigarette and leaves behind all that is bothering him for a while with every puff in the air.

He heard the phone ringing once again.

Aaaarrgghh...He always bits his lips if he is disturbed all along like this always. It's already raining the whole day in Florida and he's been wet twice already. There was so much what's bothering him nowadays. With Lisa leaving him in between the dangling life and death situation. There was so much love he'd had for her but all she cared about was to be together with the comparisons to other couples in their circle.

LISA... The beautiful word a person can be named with so much beauty in its meaning, "Oath of God". Her every word, every action would have been so pure now also with her being by my side would have already made me the best Man in the world and the best person to have found the meaning of Love. Many renowned poets and poems depict the meaning of Love in many ways, but for me, it is simple to have been in the simple and best moments for your whole life. All you need is to just listen to others with your eyes closed and listen to the beating hearts so that you don't need to speak but listen and you would get the meaning of what your partner is saying.

The proximity of Love is defined in the ways of Heart makes me think that it is not the heart but eyes which make you fall in love but not to misunderstand it with the mere vision you get through the eyes. Eyes... Eyes are ways to one's Soul is what I believe. One can lie to you but their eyes, the eyes, never lie. All you need to do is read those beautiful creations of Nature and you would be in another dimension once you get the meaning. Eyes are portals of the world of Love. Lisa used to make her eyes visible and I used to love those now and then. I never believed I would fail for such a person who can go mad about simply her hair strand not being at the right place and who gives utmost attention to her being presentable rather than being Natural. I guess that's what Lisa all about is. She was always about "Look at me, I am better than you". Why do people need to compare themselves with others when they can go underneath their skin and check for their flaws and vices and overcome those eventually?

Lisa, I saw her first in the corridor looking for someone for one of her practice sessions for a play. She was a classical Kuchipudi dancer and all her ways of life were too eccentric. She liked Arunima Kumar a lot and used to follow her in every aspect she could find out about her. Her stance while performing used to leave everyone in awe and she used to like that every time. One day while passing through the corridor, I saw her, and I fell miserably in her love at the next moment. You know, that single moment would also be enough when you understand that you are in Love. Those enthralling eyes would make anyone go on their knees and wait for the special person in that position forever. I too had already fallen for her and her eyes. Damn, those beautiful eyes.

I got into their group with me being one of the writers for the plays they were having dance performances in. Eventually, I used to spend time with her which made her fall for me (or I made her fall for me). We used to spend a lot of time together and used to discuss a lot about Art. We used to discuss a lot about "**Guillaume Apollinaire**", her favourite French poet and "**Gustave Flaubert**", my favourite one and how they revolutionized the Writing world with their creations. Art was our common string forever and we used to discuss a lot and a lot about everything. As I quote every time, I used to meet her, "You know Lisa, everything and everyone is Art. All you need to do is keep your eyes open and explore...."

We both were stunned with our mutual love for Art and Nature would make us go in the dark for days and just explore ourselves into Mother Nature. But as they say, eventually every good thing comes to an end, our love also had the finish line. While coming from one performance, an accident took her away from me and I nevertheless was broken and shattered, asked, and asked but, all she said was still shocking to me that she had lost everything and wanted me to continue to live without her. I somehow failed to understand how that can be so fast and why life has turned so cruel on me. I can't hold the pain at all and started seeing Lisa everywhere and I had to let her go....

Forever into her own life and her way of things

I let her go to be with her forever.

Life has taught me to be patient.

With love being the final action

Let her be in her world.

To find the peace, within.......

Again, this time he heard the phone, he decided, he'd receive it and yell at the person on the phone with all the might he can gather from his stomach and just go on yelling. Everything and everyone seemed miserable today to him with one more pathetically weird thing he'd seen today. One old lady, who he sees every day stuck in the wheelchair and barely can walk, was running with her hands trying to catch all the Winds and the Sunrays crushing worries on her face. This was not at all good sight for him as he can't fathom the very basic unanswered question everyone would ask, "Has she lost it?" "Is she not seeing her therapist nowadays?". All these questions are bothering him more than his unanswered questions. Human minds can play weird plays every time, every day and it can make you cry for things which are not meant to you and are far beyond your reach. The clouds covered in cray black making everything dull and miserable than it already was.

The ringing phone pissed Roy more than ever. He rushed from the balcony to pick up the phone and cursed the one on the other side. Last few days were too difficult for him to cope with the rest of the world. Lisa, his all-lifelong love has left him, and he is more than alone in the world. You know, this Life gives you everything at one moment and doesn't even wait to snatch it away from you on the next. He yelled at the receiver and said, "hello, who in the hell is so desperate not to even wait for some moments?" He heard nothing but pure silence which is in his head too nowadays. The blank head emerged from his blank mind made him realize the black hole theory he's recently gone through.

The Gravitational Singularity would make this pain go away since nothing relative to this Universe would work on that terms. The beep started coming from the Receiver and the rumbling started. The shattering voice coming from the receiver took his breath away and before even understanding the phone started to burst into the beautiful colours of rainbows. The different colours started to shift their shapes into the different anxieties Roy was having in his heads. The GAD (Generalized Anxiety Disorder), OCD (Obsessive-Compulsive Disorder), Panic Disorder, PTSD(Post-Traumatic Stress Disorder), and Social Phobia(or Social Anxiety Disorder). Each taking a humane form and dancing around his eyes with one taking Lisa's form.

Lisa what a beautiful dream he's seen and lived all along until Life was snatched out of her beautiful and gorgeous body with that weird accident that happened one night. He's been lonely since that day until today where he is seeing her alive and dancing in front of his eyes again. Although it didn't make any sense to his bare eyes and mind, he is still enjoying her being around. He's started looking into her eyes and turning it like the way he has always wanted them to be. Her beautiful eyes, he laughed at himself again remembering her eyes. Her perfect toned body, the toned breasts and her bare navel if seen can go any man on knees... He's now looking at her like she is nothing, but Eve God has created just for him.

And next moment he stopped from looking at her. He started shouting, "This is not me, this is not me." He was not able to understand the pain if it's real or what was going on in front of him was real. He started having the acute headache and blood seemed to have stopped flowing towards his brain. He was not able to think properly. He was feeling his Lifeforce coming to end with the white cloak-wearing lady stretching her hand and calling upon him to come with her to "Eden" and leave this mortal place. The beautiful Eden, where God's creations dwell and the paradise which you have seen only in those beautiful poems and creations of his favourite French poets.

The Sky was turning denser and blacker than normal. The hypnotized sky is bringing in more rains than ever in Florida. Lisa was trying to touch him and seduce him more and more. The rough day and the old wine were making the impact and he was more into her than ever. The seduction has worked, and he was moving more towards and he's started grabbing her everywhere and hurting her. Her moans were means of pleasure according to her and he was more enjoying the pain coming out her eyes.

The red colour flowing through her veins had started to ooze out and he was enjoying it with drinking the same through his favourite glass and considering him the Lucifer of her life. He's been thinking of doing this more than ever and he was finding these crucial moments for him. The more he was hitting her, the more he was enjoying hitting her and drinking her blood. The pain deep within had resurrected itself and he was enjoying it more than suffering from it.

He was into the dizziness the whole night. He was not able to neither walk properly nor think through what had happened last night. All he remembered was the cigarette, the Wine he held in his glass in his left hand and the lit cigarette he was smoking to ease the pain coming from OCD. He couldn't gather the courage to look at his torn body and shattered heart with his hands covered in blood, the blood which was freed from those controlled veins to roam around freely across the whole place and enjoy their freedom. He was now free, free from this mortal world and all he was seeing now was that his split personality mortal life had ended, and he can now freely return to the love of his Life... Lisa in the Spirit world.

Gathered people started to disperse and leave behind the body to be taken by medical staff. Police are enquiring everyone nearby and everyone is trying to save themselves with all the stories they can make out of nothing. And the telephone started ringing again...Tring Tring...Tring Tring...Tring Tring...

19

A TALE OF TWO KINDS

BY ARYAMAN KUMAR

Matt's whole world went topsy-turvy when he found himself stumbling for balance in the middle of an alleyway. He was balancing between his toes and ankles with his hands stretched out to not fall. He recognized the alley instantly, but it had an unfamiliar feel to it like this was the copy. He put his hands down when he was sure he wasn't gonna tumble down now and walked out of the alley. The street was familiar to him; it was where he lived, but the street could not be more alien. The buildings of the street were entirely different and strange; some buildings were normal while some were made to let in as much sunlight as possible, instead of blocking it out.

He remembered a grocery store which sold the best oranges Matt had ever tasted on the street, but instead of that shop was a meat shop which sold the meat of the weirdest animals he has seen. Then his eyes caught something else, something which was almost invisible but crystal clear once you notice it – there were no trees on the street. Not one piece of flora was around; it was a complete concrete jungle prevalent in shades of grey and white. Everything had a bland texture to it, with the most colourful thing being the brown buildings and the dark alleys. After the structures, his eyes were now on the people, and they weren't an exception either. It was the strangest thing he had laid eyes on, and that was saying something. He saw that some people's skin was green, and instead of hair, they had twigs and branches growing from their heads.

Matt was freaking out over what he was saying and started backing up into the alley when he stumbled into a man. "Watch where you're going!" He said in a heavy voice. He was wearing a trench coat and was carrying a briefcase in his hand, which fell when Matt stumbled into him. Matt noticed that his skin was green too, and his eyes were yellow. Instead of bending down, the man's hand extended, grabbed the briefcase, and returned to its original length. Matt felt like he was losing his sanity, losing his grip on what's real and what's not. Then it struck him. He was in a dream, or maybe a nightmare.

The dream felt more real than ever, and the nightmare was unlike any he ever had. He had had dreams about falling from a high point, drowning in a really low point, being alone and isolated from everyone and everywhere, but none were as scary as this one. "Matt?" He heard someone call him in a low tone. The man must be close to him, somewhere around him. He looked around, searching for the source and saw a homeless man lying on the pavement. He was also green skinned, but his eyes were less yellow than others. He had a lot of twigs on his cheeks and chin, which were the equivalent of a beard. He looked drunk, or sleepy, or both. "Matt, is that you?" He said again. His voice felt familiar but alien-like everything else. "Who- how do you know me?" Matt asked. "It is you." The man said and got up.

His face was recognizable to Matt; a sense of déjà vu took over him.

"You-are you Damon?"

"Yes, yes that's my name." Damon said.

"Matt, you...you're alive."

He leaned forward to hug Matt, but Matt leaned away from him and took a few steps back. He turned around and started pacing away from him. "Matt. Matt, wait." Damon said and took a few steps towards Matt. Before Matt knew it, he was running on the street being chased by a green-skinned man who claimed to be his best friend and even strangely reminded him of his best friend, even though he had twigs for the beard.

Matt ran past all the civilians he came across, even knocking some down. He knew where he was running to, since he knew exactly where what was in the street, despite it being an entirely new place for him. He ran down the street and took a left at the second intersection and from there to a construction site which was only a few meters away. He saw the construction site forming up on the horizon. Although it was different from what he remembered, it was still exactly where it was. It was fenced from every side except for a few feet wide entrances from where Matt entered the site. The construction wasn't happening at that time and no one was around, so no one stopped Matt from entering the building and climbing a few floors. He could feel the green-skinned man chasing him, gaining and losing him at times. Damon climbed up the stairs in pursuit of Matt.

He didn't know why he was running from him, but he had bigger questions than just that. Although it was Matt he had known and grown up with, he still felt different to him. The last time he had seen him he had never thought he would ever get a chance to ever see him again, or whether he even wanted to see him again or not. It had been so long since that day he honestly couldn't remember how he felt about him anymore. His anger and rage had melted away and was now replaced by only emptiness and loneliness. Damon saw Matt go through a door, and he followed him inside. Inside he was taken aback when he saw Matt holding a steel rod aimed at Damon's head, but he didn't intend to use it, Damon could tell.

"Stay back, stay the hell back." Matt swore.

"Whoa whoa calm down calm down, I'm not here to hurt or kill you, Matt."

"How do you know me?!"

"Same way you know who I am, it's me, Damon. Matt, I forgive you for what you did, everything was madness, no wonder you cracked."

"What the hell are you talking about? You're not the Damon I know, you can't be."

"Okay I think I know what's going on here, it's a crazy idea, but I did see you vaporize out of thin air, so who am I to talk about crazy?"

"What the hell are you talking about?"

"Just listen to me. You may be from some other world or a...parallel universe...where you had a friend, Damon, just like I had a friend Matt. But now, somehow, you've been transported over to this universe."

Matt lowered the rod.

"That's weirdly accurate."

"Well, I was always interested in parallel universes so..."

"Okay, I believe you. But I'll still keep this in case you try something."

"Yeah, that's fine by me."

"Also...I didn't 'had' a friend, I 'have' a friend named Damon." Damon sighed.

"Oh." "What happened to...um...your Matt?"

Matt said, not believing what he was saying. "I don't think you wanna know."

"Oh, okay." Matt nodded his head.

"Also, like, what are you? Why are you like a plant?"

"I'm a plantoid, of course."

"A what?"

"A plantoid." Damon sighed.

"They don't have plantoids in your universe, do they?"

"No, they don't. I still don't get what you are, like an alien species or something?"

"No, I'm not an alien." Damon said in an offended tone.

"We evolved from simple plants during the same times humans evolved. There were more with us, you know, who evolved. Not just chimps and some random plants. It was like several species gained sentience altogether. But they were all driven to extinction, and in the end, there were only you humans and us plantoids."

"That's...weird. How did so many species evolve together?"

"People call it an unnatural phenomenon. Matt used to say all phenomena are unnatural-"

"-until they occur."

"Yes, forgot you were him."

"So that's why you guys don't have any grocery stores and trees."

"That'll be unethical, yeah."

They both were chuckling and getting along now. Matt's grip on the rod had loosened a lot by now, as it felt like he was talking to an old friend of his instead of someone he was running from a while ago. They both sat down, cross-legged, and talked for a little while longer.

"How is my human counterpart?"

"Well, not different from you, actually, only in appearance." Matt said.

"Where is my counterpart? Is he a human or a plantoid?"

"He was a human." Damon said, upset.

"Okay, you gotta tell me now, what happened to me? Am I dead? And what did I do? Why were you forgiving me?"

Damon's head hung down, he was visibly distressed, but Matt didn't seem to care. He wanted to know what happened to him.

"Okay...okay I'll tell you." Damon nodded.

"This happened around two years ago when Matt and I joined the War. The War was like a world war or something, you know?"

"Of course, I know we have two of them."

"Yeah, we got involved in this war. A country was trying to exterminate all the humans in their country, and that situation escalated, and many countries got involved in it. Anyway, we were in the war the longest in our platoon. We saw between two hundred and three hundred days in combat, longer than anyone there. Suffice it to say, we saw a lot of things together. The war was...devastating. I felt like a traitor for fighting people of my species, it just wasn't fair. And during all this, something was going on with Matt, I could tell that, something that wasn't right. One day we got some info that some POWs were kept in a farmhouse located in a small town. Matt and I were selected for their rescue mission. The journey to the town and then to the farmhouse was relatively easier than other times, which led us to believe that most of the forces were inside the farmhouse. Matt decided to lead a team inside while I waited outside with some people. I remember when I heard the shots of the guns and the bullets ricocheting inside the farmhouse when Matt entered it.

One could tell that something wasn't right, something was amiss. So I decided to check the place out. Inside, it was clear what had happened. The POWs, mostly plantoids, were killed, and so were all of the soldiers. And it was clear who did that – Matt. He was the only one alive there, but gravely injured."

Matt didn't say anything for a moment.

"Why would... Matt...do that?"

"He was a human, the prisoners and most of the soldiers were plantoids. The war just drove him mad; he started thinking that all plantoids were his enemies, including me." Matt widened his eyes.

"He tried to shoot at me, but his gun was empty. I was...enraged at that moment. I didn't even mercy-kill him; I just left him to succumb to his injuries, my own best friend."

Damon looked at Matt. "It's all nonsense, I know, but this is what happened."

"Kinda weird hearing about my death, you know." Matt chuckled.

"Your world is better than ours, you know. You people aren't separated from each other like we all are."

"Is it though? We don't have anything to separate us, but...we're not together. We have wars too, trust me we do, and it sucks, it all sucks. So, our world...not so different from your bro, it's not better at all."

They sat there for a while staring out into the wall, zoned out in their thoughts and worlds.

"What will you do now?" Damon asked.

"I don't care."

MEET THE CO-AUTHORS

Celestina Copil

Coffee, solitude, and a laptop is everything Celestina needs to start writing. 16-year-old Romanian girl often spends her nights listening to the whispers of the stars (very few of which are visible, unfortunately) that inspire her. Playing with words is her way of expressing her soul.

Urvi Dhruva

Urvi Dhruva has big plans in her tiny head. She would describe herself as raita; khatta, meetha and all over the place. She likes everything cheesy (except pick-up lines). Until she can figure out mind-reading, she will stick to reading books.

Isheta Boruah

Isheta Boruah, the 20-year-old writer, hails from Assam, Guwahati. Apart from writing she also has a keen interest in Legal aspects and has interned and put her hands-on sectors encircling Human Rights, Intellectual Property Rights, Criminal and Civil Law, and has also wrote and published Research Papers pertaining to Human Rights facets. She is currently pursuing BA.LLB Honours from National Law University and Judicial Academy, Assam. She is also working as an Editor for couple of Magazine and E-newspaper. She also has her hands-on swimming and has bagged laurel encircling the area.

Prathibha Srinivasan

Meet Prathibha, an architect turned part-time writer. Her favourite things/people in the world are her mom, chocolate, and books, in that order. She stays in a dream world more than 90% of the time and when forced to come back to the real world can get quite cantankerous. She also loves to travel but considers herself a home bird, contrary being her middle name. She aims to become a full-fledged writer, once she gets rid of the pesky affliction called procrastination.

Shubha Pai

Literature to cricket, academics to movies, mythology to quantum physics, politics to DC, these are just a few of the varied and weird combinations of Shubha's interests. Apart from studying, reading, watching, and eating, in her free time, Shubha also manages to save the world with her humour.

Adithya AJ

An abstraction of a voyager of greys that drift beyond horizons of half-thoughts and have-beens, an accident of sentience and irresoluteness, an eternity too late to the cosmos, for 'unbelonging' is the only emotion that mankind stirs within this interrobang that is A.J. and his poetry on "The Inked Dreams"

Shivangi Gupta

Shivangi is a partial engineer by day, an enigmatic writer by night. A hoarder of pictures, bookmarks and poetry, clichés are her guilty pleasure. She shoots brilliant puns when the stars align and believes that although actions speak louder than words, words are quite loud if you're willing to listen.

Akshitha Gajanand

Akshitha Gajanand is a happy go lucky girl who wears her heart on sleeve and carries a positive vibe. She's a good listener as she adores the fact that everyone has a different story to tell. She's also a medical student who loves to explore and made her debut in the book world with the story 'Maybe Somewhere Else'.

Siddhanth Raju

Hello dear readers,

It was my first time attempting to write something professional I hope you like it, there is no moral there is no end just trust in the Mechanics of this universe and take a step.

Amy Grace

A big-time dreamer. She always dreams of hugging clouds and the untamed Lion. The innocence and fluffiness of the clouds besides the fierceness and boldness of the Lion always remind her that words have power. Blessed and witty enough to use both of these extremes well.

C.L. Williams

C.L. Williams is an international bestselling author living in central Virginia. He's written eight poetry books, five novellas, one novel, and a contributor to a multitude of anthologies. When not writing, C.L. Williams is posting videos on his YouTube channel or reading the works of fellow independent authors.

Harsha Shinde

Harsha is a 16-year-old, her world revolves around fiction and fantasy. She is driven by curiosity and vouches for, indulging in books and words can precisely create our own little world. Connect with her through her Instagram page *@goldenhourwritings* where she pins down her thoughts.

Raga Lahari

Lahari is a 20-year-old aspiring writer from Hyderabad who studied BA Psychology, Journalism and Literature. Her style of expression is enthralling. Her literature is a psychological reflection of the world, real or imagined. It makes her readers introspective and interestingly contemplative while enjoying their read.

Bibin K Babu

Bibin K Babu, a 21-year-old introverted ambivert. His limitation of exploring the universe outside does not affect him from exploring the one within. He does not go with the term writer, rather someone who likes to occasionally jot down his weird yet captivating reveries.

Nikita K

Nikita is a Management Consultant currently working in Bangalore. While she loves the outdoors and travelling, she has always found solace in literature and art. She dabbles in creative writing to escape the mundane and the monotonous and hopes her words can do the same for her readers.

Pravallika Kadiri

Pravallika is a 19-year-old management student who likes her thoughts to be on a paper rather than her mind either by writing or painting. She believes that art has the power to heal people and also that everything in this universe happens for a reason.

Rasagya Gade

Rasagya is a 15-year-old 11th grade student and Kuchipudi dancer from Hyderabad with a strong and creative mind. She likes to share about social equality through creative stories.

Tushar Dudhade

Tushar, son of Mr. Trimbak Dudhade and Mrs. Surekha Dudhade is born and brought up in Maharashtra state of India. Software Developer by profession, Tushar is an avid Reader, Trekker, and an old Soul, who strives to make his parents proud and live his life to the fullest.

Aryaman Kumar

Aryaman Kumar was born in 2002 in Gurugram. Growing up, he was fascinated with football, but this interest was soon replaced by a passion for ideas and writing. Aryaman, who started writing in 6th grade, is now a first-year college student, and has a knack for sarcasm. If he isn't spending time with his friends and family, you can almost always find him binge-watching a show (Breaking Bad is his personal favourite). A Tale Of Two Kinds is Aryaman's first story to be published.

OUR STORY

We're all on a Journey, and our "Writers" have made it Beautiful.

A dreamcatcher is an object made with feathers and strings, essentially used as lucky charms in many parts of the world. The same way, Inkfeathers brings together writers, editors, and artists together to form a dreamcatcher that works in favour for the young writers and readers and if you're positive about it, it may bring you luck as well.

We at Inkfeathers are connected to thousands of writers globally, who believe in the magic of telling stories. This stream of connectivity with the writers, the fact that everyone has a unique detail or edge to their story makes Inkfeathers proud to partner with these young literary as well as collaborative minds.

Back in 2013, our founders came together to form an offline group for their love of literature, and this formed collaborative energy with many young literature-wounded minds which eventually led these offline meetings to stand-ups, storytelling events, poetry slams, meet-ups to share experiences and many others. In 2016, Inkfeathers finally launched as the brand project under one Private Limited Company. This expanded opportunity gave a number of possibilities and a new way to expand our support for writers.

This dream of wanting to bring together writers as well as readers has come true beyond measure as writers connect to us from countries like United States, United Kingdom, Canada each day to bring their stories to life.

From 2020, we are extremely delighted to provide you our website (www.inkfeathers.com) where all your queries can be resolved about our self-publishing process and latest anthologies. You can get hold of the latest updates on anthologies, events, offers, new book releases and so much more here. You can go ahead and order a book from our bookstore to get a taste of our mindful curation of stories and poems.

Inkfeathers Publishing family encourages you to really put your feelings out there in words for the world to see, in order to have a common ground to grow mutually. We are a creative platform for all those seeking literary help in terms of having their words published.

Believe us, publishing a book is not easy, but we come to a writer's rescue at each phase of having their book in print in terms of Editing, Designing, Branding, Marketing and all the other work that goes behind until you have a printed copy in your hands for Distribution. Together, it couldn't have been any easier. We will be there for you, to help you turn your manuscript into a freshly bound book that sells off the glass bookshelves.

With Love,
Inkfeathers Publishing

INKFEATHERS PUBLISHING

India's Most Author Friendly Publishing House

Stay updated about latest books, anthologies, events, exclusive offers, contests, product giveaways and other things that we do to support authors.

f   Inkfeathers Publishing

◉   @InkfeathersPublishing

🐦   @_Inkfeathers

in   @Inkfeathers

🌐   Inkfeathers.com

We'd love to connect with you!